# THE SECRETS BEHIND CLOSED DOORS

*Niveah Jewell*

iUniverse, Inc.
New York Bloomington

This is a work of fiction. All of the characters, names, incidents,
organizations, and dialogue in this novel are either the products
of the author's imagination or are used fictitiously.

iUniverse books may be ordered through booksellers or by contacting:

iUniverse
1663 Liberty Drive
Bloomington, IN 47403
www.iuniverse.com
1-800-Authors (1-800-288-4677)

ISBN: 978-1-4401-8479-6 (sc)
ISBN: 978-1-4401-8478-9 (ebook)

Printed in the United States of America

iUniverse rev. date: 10/22/2009

When life seems to be all you can bear
And you feel there is no more to spare
When you have shed your last tear
And you feel you can tarry no more
Reach for your hope
Reach for the comforter
God surely cares


Life enriches a young girl's life that has suffered sexual, emotional and physical abuse and learns to rid her heart of hatred and learns to love. For many years throughout my life I have carried a heavy heart for the abused and pray each day for their safety and redemption of their perpetrators. I offer you the hope I learned to cling to.

I dedicate this book to my special friends in LA and family and friends that have supported me along the way.

# Chapter One

THE SKIES WERE CLEAR with a thick morning smoky haze while the greenery lay embedded throughout the mountains as far as the eye could see. The cool breeze embraced every thought as it rustled through the air. Niveah sat on her porch early in the morning breathing in the refreshing scent of pine and feeling the warmth that she loved about the mountains as she recalled her secret thoughts of her childhood in a small suburban town in Ohio. She meditated with a silent harmonious heart for other families that had hidden secrets as her thoughts drifted to the deepest closed doors of her mind's eye as she often did when she was alone.

"Funny how things work out in life's journey's and how it all comes together as one endearing destiny," she chuckled aloud, sipping her tea.

The summer of 1977 the bluish skies glistened with the promising of rain showers. The aroma of mothers' rose garden filled the house with a soothing comfort as I curled up on the soft plush leather couch taking in all the pleasantness the atmosphere offered while I wrote all the memories that I would someday want to recall in my journal. Secretly on the pages I would write of journey's I would take across the globe and careful not to leave out my desires I wanted to accomplish when I grew up.

Interrupting the calmness of the moment the phone rang.

"Hello sweetness, can you baby-sit while I clean up the backyard?" asked the voice of my favorite uncle.

"Oh my God, yes!" I shouted.

"I will ask my mother." I replied. With excitement I went to receive permission. I was eleven and felt important that I would be considered to fulfill the task.

"Mom, can I please go baby-sit my little cousin?" I pleaded.

My mother recognized my enthusiasm and gladly took the phone to make the arrangements with my uncle. Mother hung up the phone and skeptically announced that I would be allowed to baby-sit and permitted me to spend the night.

I scampered off to pack an overnight bag. I was excited and hurriedly grabbed a bathing suit, a complete change of clothes and my favorite pair of pajamas. I took my bag for inspection and told her about the twenty-five dollars that I was going to earn. I was gleaming with excitement and included her in on the money stash I had hidden for a trip to an African Safari when I grew up. She didn't seem too surprised for I was the adventurous child with a never-ending imagination.

Mother drove me to the country to my aunt and uncle's house. We discussed several different activities that I could do to occupy the rambunctious child. The summer heat was still lingering so swimming was the main idea.

Immediately upon arrival I changed to my bathing suit and prepared the toddler for the pool.

Meanwhile mom addressed concerns with my uncle the time I was expected to be home the next day.

Mother watched from a distance as I played with the little boy in the pool. I assured her I would be okay and blew her a good-bye kiss. She smiled and waved as she caught my kiss in mid-air and drove away.

I pushed the toddler around the pool in his float. He laughed and kicked his feet. I remember thinking how much fun babysitting was going to be although I was silently counting the dollars that I could make.

After playing for a couple of hours in the pool, the youngster had begun to get cranky and whiny. I remembered my mother explaining to warm the bottle before bedtime. So without hesitation I gathered him up close to me with one arm as I attempted to climb out of the pool however I kept slipping. With every slip was a splash and for every splash was a whimper from the baby.

Admitting defeat, I yelled for, "Help!"

My uncle came to the rescue.

Apologetically I explained the situation as I lifted the screaming toddler over the side of the pool to his daddy.

My uncle started walking away but turned to me instead, "You can stay in the pool longer if you want to. I am through with the yard work and I will take the little tyke inside."

"That's great!" and I jumped back in the pool. I must have swum for a really long time because it had gotten completely dark. I climbed out of the pool hurriedly and ran down the lit sidewalk that led to the backdoor.

My uncle greeted me in the hallway with an oversized towel held out.

"Here sweetness, Go ahead and slip out of that wet suit, you don't want to make Auntie mad for dripping all over the floor. Do you?"

"No I sure don't but you will see me." I said hesitantly.

"No I promise not to peek." he reassured me.

He held the towel close to me and insisted for me to hurry. Awkwardly and discreetly I slipped off the wet suit and grabbed the towel tightly around me and secured it with a knot across my chest. I moved towards the drying rack and draped my suit over it as my uncle moved close up behind me and in a commanding whisper instructed me to go take a hot shower. I listened intensely and felt scared and a strange queasiness in my stomach. I pushed away from him and ran off through the dark candle-lit house.

"Take a quick shower and wash all that chlorine from your body" he yelled at me from the other end of the hall.

I felt so strange and the sick feeling I started getting had turned into a huge ball in the pit of my stomach. I was scared and oddly enough I didn't know why. I turned the door knob quickly and closed the bathroom door tightly as I leaned up against the door as to stay hidden. My heart raced as I panted to catch my breath. I felt so strangely weird. I looked around the bathroom and the dim nightlight outlined the light-switch so I reached for it and flipped it on slowly as if I were expecting someone to be in the brightness. Why was I so scared and jumpy? I stood at the edge of the marble tub to warm the shower. I pulled the golden shower curtain back to safeguard the floor from getting wet. I removed the towel that I was still wearing tightly wrapped around me and draped it on the towel rack below the shelf that held praying hands and a framed note that read "have a nice safe day as you begin each day". I giggled to myself and what about the night-time. I just didn't feel safe and oddly felt as if I had done something wrong. I got a clean towel from the linen shelf and laid it near the tub and climbed into the marbled tub to indulge in a hot shower.

The longer I indulged in the warm water the calmer I became. My fingertips were becoming shriveled up like a prune and the hot water was turning cold so I rinsed the soap off for the third time and turned the water off.

I finished with my hot soothing shower and I peeked around the shower curtain to reach for my drying towel but to my surprise I could see my uncle's reflection in the misty mirror. His slender shadow was moving closer to the shower and his hand reached for the shower curtain. Scared and embarrassed I moved to the far side of the stall as the shower curtain was flung open to expose my nakedness to the eyes of a man. Shamefully I tried to cover myself as I lowered my head in embarrassment.

I hugged my body with my arms draped across my body to cover the private parts and my eyes were fixated on my toes, while I listened to a gruff tone of my uncle, commanding me to get out of the shower and to put on a gown he had laid out for me.

I only nodded with obedience to the adult that stood before me.

Reaching to lift my face up at his he kissed my lips and said, "You are such a good girl."

I tried to back up closer to the cold tiled wall but I was as close as I could get and there was no place for me to hide myself. My head drooped down in fear and shame and I never took my eyes off my feet. I was embarrassed and felt ashamed with some kind of odd feeling of guilt.

He walked out the bathroom and slammed the door behind him. I jumped out from the shower to check the door and once I knew it was secured I slid to the floor and cried. I held my face in my hands and drew my knees up close to my chest as I sat scared and alone remaining clueless of what to do next. I sniffled and wiped the tears away from my eyes. Thinking he would come back if I didn't hurry.

I dried off and held the gown up to me that my uncle had insisted that I was to put on. I had never seen a gown that was see through and that had fancy lace. I was scared that I would be in trouble for putting it on but it was obvious I would be in trouble for not doing so. I obeyed and followed the instructions that were given to me.

After I got the gown on I looked in the mirror and saw my nudity revealed and wondered why people bothered wearing a gown made like that. Then I thought to myself my mom would never allow me to wear this and suddenly I began to feel that same weird feeling that I just had in the shower of guilt and shame. I wasn't doing anything wrong or was I?

Then I remembered the gown my aunt and uncle had bought me last Christmas. It was short, red and white with ruffles that tied together with a ribbon. The panties matched with ruffle sequence. Although I wasn't allowed to wear it my parents allowed me to keep it in a hope box. So my reasoning was that if I could keep the other one then this one would be okay too and I wouldn't get into trouble. My rationalizing didn't make me feel better but it did make sense to do as I was told to do.

My thoughts were interrupted by my uncle calling for me, "Pizza getting cold! Hurry up!"

My robe had been removed from the bathroom. Panic stricken I fumbled about the bathroom closet looking for an extra large towel to wrap around me. I wrapped the towel around me tightly and exited the bathroom.

"Hmmm, I am coming; I can't find my robe." I stuttered quietly.

"You don't need it! Now get in here and eat before you wake the baby up!" My uncle answered with a command. His tone of voice made me feel like I was about to get in trouble. I was scared and unsure of what to do. So I obeyed.

I went to the living room and sat on the far end of the couch attempting to cover my private parts that I felt were exposed.

"I want to go home!" I said as I grabbed a piece of pizza.

"No! You're not allowed to yet!" he snapped as he slid to my end of the couch.

"Sweetness, you and me are going to watch movies and have fun before your boring auntie get's here and spoils the fun."

Startled by the touch of a hand on my shoulder, I dropped my pizza and ran off to the bedroom that I was to share with my little cousin. I was scared and just wanted to call my mom. Instead, knowing I wasn't allowed to, I just crawled quietly under the blankets. Tearfully I scooted up against the wall and curled up in a ball. I pulled the covers over my face and thought if I couldn't be seen I would be okay.

Meanwhile, my aunt arrived home from work. I could hear shouting from the next room but unable to make out the words being said. A door slammed and everything was quiet. Alarmed by the squeaky sound from the floor I knew someone was coming towards the shut

bedroom door where I lay lifeless. Slowly turning the doorknob someone entered the room. It was him. It was my uncle. I recognized the scent of old spice and the slender body shadow cast onto the wall although it was dark in the room the bright nightlight and the moonlight shining in through the window confirmed my uncle's presence. I lied still in my fear and drowning in my tears. I thought to myself he will leave as soon as he witnessed the child slept soundly in his crib and that I was fast asleep in my own bed. I was careful not to make a sound and wanting to scream but only too scared to do so.

I felt body weight set on the side of the bed and my eyes clinched shut while he tugged at my blankets until my hidden body was revealed. The shadows of my uncle were highlighted on the wall as he motioned for me to be silent. I was scared and drew my knees tight into my chest.

"You are a special niece," he said. His hands were cold on my body as he touched forbidden places. I cried aloud and he placed his hand snuggly over my mouth. I began too sniffle and his hand covered my mouth tighter. I felt as if I couldn't breathe.

His free hand freely roamed over my legs pressing my knees downward away from my chest forcing my knees apart. Tears rolled down my cheeks as I held my breath, my eyes closed tightly so I couldn't witness the man who fondled my innocent body. I began squirming closer to the wall but he only kept pulling me back to the edge of the bed where my body kept meeting his wandering hands. His breath smelled of stale smoke and beer as he bent towards my face to kiss my forehead. I attempted, once again, to scoot next to the wall but he only pulled me roughly towards him. My tears rushed from my eyes and dripped over his hand that that held my screams silently in.

His free-hand continued to go up and down my legs and finally in between my thighs to my most private part of my body. He continued touching my body in the deepest darkest corner of the room against my will. As he took my hand and placed his penis in it he made weird moans as he moved his hand up and down over mine. I closed my eyes and let the tears fall. A strange yucky slime streamed over my hand as he bent over my lifeless body and laid his head over my chest. He kissed my cheek then rubbed his slimy hand over my formed breast. His hand grew tighter over my mouth and I felt as if I were suffocating under his large hand.

Once again he kissed my forehead and cheek and whispered, "My sweetness, don't make a sound when I take my hand away from your mouth. You know we had to be quiet while we had our fun so the baby wouldn't wake up."

I only nodded in silence. I was scared and trembled in fear.

My uncle stood from the tiny bed I laid in and then kissed me on the cheek. I could see the dark shadow of him moving about the room to check on the baby before he finally left the room.

My stomach was sick and I cried until I vomited on myself.

"I want my mommy," I screamed out.

My aunt came running into the room, shouting, "It will be okay. It's too late at night to call your mom and she would be mad if we woke her up. You are just having a bad dream." She cradled me up in her arms and wiped my tears. Auntie continued comforting me with kind words of how much she loved me and a soothing humming sound. She stood and tucked the covers tightly around me and kissed me good-night on the forehead.

She turned to the door and stopped to bend down to whisper to me, "It will be okay but you shouldn't have had worn that gown. This will be our little secret and everything is alright now. Go to sleep,"

My auntie kissed me goodnight once again and quickly walked to the door and closed it securely behind her.

I turned to the wall and scooted up as close to it as I could and cried myself to sleep.

Morning didn't come soon enough. I hurriedly dressed and gathered my belongings. I was eager to go home.

I exited the bedroom I occupied and turned to shut the door as to shut the secrets behind the closed door.

I could hear chatter of voices from the next room and discretely announced I was ready to go home.

Ignoring my announced request they only offered me breakfast and I politely refused. I felt too sick at my stomach to think about eating. I sat quietly fiddling with my bag and twirling a loose string on my shirt.

It was late morning before we left to go to my house. The ride was quieter and seemed longer than usual. The adults occasionally exchanged words concerning their errands that needed to be done. The baby sat staring out the window as to not miss a passing sight. I sat close to the door ready to escape as soon as the chance arisen.

Finally, my house was in view and I clenched the door handle tightly. I would be ready for a quick escape, I thought to myself.

My aunt said to me, "I will call your mom later to arrange for you to come next Friday to stay with us."

I hissed at her disobediently with a no thank you. With a tight squeeze to my arm she insisted that I would be babysitting on Friday evenings. I felt a distinct uneasiness of fear and ran towards the house where my mother stood waiting for me.

I ran by mother with a quick hello and a peck on the cheek and went straight to my room where I knew for certain no harm would come to me. I flopped down in the floor in front of my mirror where my friend always waited for me. Me!

I sat crossed legged on the floor and spoke aloud to myself. I imagined aloud of growing up and going far, far away. I wanted to hide in a jungle where no one would find me and no people to harm me. I imagined sitting on tree limbs with leopards purring at my feet. I would swim in rivers with crocodiles and make friends with the anaconda's. I would explore the waterfalls with such intensity to notice each drop of water and each color that would sparkle through. Most of all I just wanted to be alone so no one could harm me again. I wanted to be happy and free from secrets.

My happy-land was interrupted by mother's sweet voice, "Sis, are you okay? Did you have fun?"

"Yes everything is alright. I just want to take a nap that's all," I replied.

Over the next few months I continued to baby-sit out of fear of questions that might be asked and I somehow believed my parents would be disappointed in me if they were to ever know of the forbidden secret. After all, my aunt told me that my parent's would be mad at me and I trusted her.

Mother began to address concern that I wasn't spending enough time with my friends. I started dropping my love for sports and replacing game time with solitaire. I didn't ride my bike anymore. I only washed it and put it away. I began to have nightmares and sleepwalk.

I was scared to say anything and began to feel like I wasn't a good daughter. I developed a fear of every shadow made during the night. I wanted to go to sleep and never wake up.

Finally the following spring my mother asked if I would rather volunteer at the hospital instead of babysitting all the time. I gladly accepted.

Nearly a year passed and I thought of the incidences with my uncle less and less. I excelled at school and in sports once again. However, I still was skeptical of being around a lot of people. I remained popular but at the same time I felt a sense of not belonging. I would sit in a crowd and listen to the chitchat and feel loneliness that would consume me. I always felt like they knew my dirty secrets and was judging me. I became obsessed with being the perfect child.

I didn't want my parents to view me as anything less than their prideful joy. The words of my aunt haunted me so clearly: they will be mad at you, you will be in trouble. I couldn't disappoint my parents that I loved so dearly.I had become a young teen that was afraid of existing with the living and torn apart within myself of being happy.

Months passed by and the monster growing inside of me had started to become distant and small.

I became involved at school once again. I wrote history plays and directed them for the drama club to perform. I participated in choir and became the notorious French Club president. I was back on top of success as editor of the school paper. I excelled with volunteer work and morbidly driven by trauma. Life as a growing teenager was good. I was happy again.

However, one summer afternoon my mother announced at the dinner table that my aunt and uncle were moving from the country closer to us. We were going to visit with them after dinner. Immediately, I felt sick and violated. My emotions were in complete turmoil and my newly found happiness was in sudden doom.

My siblings and cousins raced to the car while I tagged along slowly bringing up the rear.

I panicked with fear as my mind ran a horror picture of the forbidden incidences. I didn't want to go but I knew there would be a lot of questions since it were a known fact that they were my favorite aunt and uncle. I had to remain calm and quiet and pull through the excitement scene. I reassured myself that I would be okay because I wouldn't be left alone.

Upon arrival to my relative's new home a sudden eeriness came over me as we were greeted at the front door by the whole family. My mom and aunt headed to the kitchen to busy themselves with unpacking boxes. All of us six children were instructed to go upstairs to the playroom. My dreadful uncle remained outside. I kept thinking we wouldn't be here long. We will just play a little while and then we will be leaving.

Our playtime was interrupted by heavy footsteps and a gruff voice saying, "Go outside and play!"

It was my treacherous uncle coming up the stairs. What did he want?

We all put the toys away and each of us older children took the hand of a younger child and headed for the stairwell. I mingled in line quickly but was pulled aside as everyone else went down the stairs noisily.

My uncle held my arms firmly and glared at me sternly. With unspoken words I knew it was best to not make a scene. Obediently, I stood still in my fear. I was afraid to stand still but afraid to make a ruckus.

Once everyone was clear from eyesight my uncle swung me around in front of him. He groped my developed breasts and told me I had been a bad girl for refusing to baby sit all this time. I kicked at him and swung my arms violently until I broke his hold. Then I ran to the steps where he caught me again. He forced me against the wall and held me in place with his body weight while he grabbed my face and forced his lips on mine. He reeked of a familiar smell of liquor and laughed grotesquely. I spit in his face and as he stepped back to wipe it off then I squirmed loose from his hold. I ran down the rest of the step's skipping a few and out the front door I went. I felt dirty, ashamed and queasy. I wanted to go home. I didn't look back and only heard the slamming door as I stayed focused on the car. I had to get to it and lock myself in. I was breathing so hard I could hardly catch my breath. Thoughts of the prior two years raced through my mind like a movie reel playing. My whole body was wet from sweat and tears fell from my eyes uncontrollably.

The other children had been playing in the side yard and came running to the commotion they heard.

"Are you alright? What's wrong?" they asked.

"I am sick! Get my mom!" I screamed.

Two of the younger children went to get my mother and we left shortly after that. Several attempts were made on my mother's behalf to find out what was wrong. I made no offers to answer other than I wanted to go home.

I closed my eyes and drifted to that private jungle where I was protected and happy. My heart slowly calmed and my mind was resting. My insides were coming together where they had felt like they broke into. I was secure and safe in my haven. Meanwhile I fell apart on the outside I cried and screamed out of control until I vomited.

The drive from hell ended as mother pulled in the driveway. Everyone quickly got out with the exception of me. I sat in hesitation staring down at my lap that was filled with mucous and the hands that held the afternoon's lunch and dinner. I felt like I couldn't go any further and just wanted to sit still as everything else around me moved about around me.

Mother was inquisitive with so many questions. I never answered only discreetly shrugged a shoulder and insisted I was just sick. However I still managed to hold on to the secret with my whole being instead of screaming it out like I wanted to.

Mother assisted me to the house and provided me with showering necessities. I felt so dizzy and wobbly as I stood and let the hot water rinse the filthy feelings I had surrounding me deep inside me. I drifted into a trance of complete disparity while I tried to bring into focus of the awareness that bound me. The contamination I felt that was on my body was stuck to me with an ugly foul odor that I couldn't eliminate and I scrubbed my body intensely and just cried.

I stared at body's nakedness in hopes that it would float down the drain pipes and go away. My early developed body seemed to only cause a lot of trouble that I didn't totally understand. My body began to look ugly to me especially the size of my young breast's. Why did boy's and grown men want to touch them anyway?

The hot water finally ran out and I sat down on the shower floor watching as the water ran through the drain. I imagined that every drip was of the haunting that dwelt deep within and wondered if my nightmare could disappear down the drain too.

I got out and dried off quickly then dressed for bed. I only wanted to sleep to never be awakened again..

I went to my room and slipped under the covers. The heap of stuffed animals made me feel safe as I surrounded myself with them .I hugged up my covers close to me as I cried myself to an exhausted slumber.

I awoke sometime that evening to my parent's shouting voices. Shouting was never permitted so I listened intensely. Although the words spoken were unclear I could tell that the two of them were distinctively angry. Then I heard clearly my mother's soft voice announce, "Something has happened to her."

I knew I was the topic of their anger just as my aunt had predicted.

Mother's gentle footsteps began to climb the stairs to my room. My heart began to race and it was as if I couldn't breathe. I knew mom was coming to get answers for my longtime bizarre behavior. I lie very still and quiet. I was scared and didn't know what to do so I closed my eyes tightly to pretend that I was sleeping. Gently mom tapped me on the shoulder. I had already become teary eyed and slowly I turned towards her.

"What has happened to my innocent little girl?" she asked.

"Has someone touched you?" mother asked directly.

I couldn't speak. I just wrapped my arms around her as she hugged me close. She cradled me up as if I were once again her infant and assured me that no one was going to ever hurt me again. My body trembled with relief of sobs rolling down my face and I felt safe. I never spoke only answered the questions she asked with an occasional shrug or nod. She sat me up on the bed beside her and stroked my hair until the tears subsided.

"Would you like for me to bring you anything?" mother asked.

I gave a silent answer and only nodded indicating no.

I heard my mother's footsteps hurry down the stairs and she bellowed into a loud cry. I imagined my father consoling her against him with a strong force.

The door slammed and a car spun from the driveway. Where were they going? I wondered.

I was alone in the house and everything was quiet. I lied back on the bed and fell asleep.

Some hours later my parents returned home. Startled from peaceful rest I could hear my father's angry voice.

"No one is to go near those people ever again!" he commanded.

I could hear their heartache through the tears they shed for me that dreary day.

Later I overheard the replay of the confrontation my parents had with the involved family members. The words that were used by my aunt and grandma were overbearing for me. They had referred to me as a slut, bitch, whore, liar and jezebel. Although I didn't know what was meant by most of the words I knew it wasn't good.

I recall feeling a painful loss wrapped in a bundle of shame, rejection and embarrassment. I was so confused but uncertain of what the confusion really was. I was certain that I had caused a lot of trouble, grief and heartache for my family. While at the same time I knew I hadn't done anything wrong. All I knew for certain and with clarity was those that professed to have loved me all my life and I in return adored them had openly rejected me and ridiculed me. I felt like an outcast. It was as if my existence held no purpose.

Months following, I would cry to an extreme. Then one day I just stopped. I wasn't happy or sad just numb within my being.

I often recognized a distinct sadness in my mother and felt totally responsible due to my revealed secret. I would overhear her prayers to reunite our broken family and I vowed to myself that I would make it up to her by excelling as her daughter. I would make her so proud of me she wouldn't have time to be sad and lonely.

I excelled in all my academic classes. I became lead vocalist in choir. I spent my spare time producing and writing documentaries and promoting them for educational aids. I stayed extremely busy and became a highly decorated student. I was very popular with the whole student body but felt as if I were a withering spring flower deep inside my soul. It never seemed to matter how much I accomplished I always felt like it wasn't enough. I wasn't happy with myself and believed that no one else could be happy and pleased with me either.

# Chapter Two

ONE DAY I WAS eye to eye with a local boy, he offered to carry my book bag.

We became study buddies. Sometimes we would ride bikes or go on short hikes together. He would call me every night at nine o'clock. We became best of friends. We would sneak and hold hands and add a kiss here and there. He would tell me I was prettier than any other girl he knew. He made me feel special. I liked him and he liked me. I would feel all fuzzy and warm inside whenever he would be near me. My lifetime friend was my rescuer from my secret pain. Summer came and we started to refer to each other as boyfriend and girlfriend. It was exciting until he started pressuring me for sex. I would say no and he would keep persisting. Eventually, he added that it was no big deal and everyone did it so we should too. However, the old haunting nightmares of my uncle's abuse towards me started to emerge. The whole ordeal of my boyfriend talking about sex made the familiar sick feeling reappear in my stomach.

One late night conversation on the phone I began to cry and I confided my secret. He began apologizing to me immediately and insisted he would never make me sad. I thought I would always trust him.

He said, "I love you!" the magical words were spoken.

"I would have never brought sex up if I would have known. I would have treated you differently, I'm so sorry." he said comforting me.

I hung on every word in silence and with a small stream of tears I believed every word.

Meanwhile his friends kept nudging him about sex and because I kept refusing he eventually broke up with me, but not without first calling me the same demeaning names that my grandparents, aunt and uncle had referred to me as being many months prior.

He sought out a girl that would say yes to sex and she became pregnant.

I was confused with the idea that seemed to be a fact: people say they love you then call you names and hurt your feelings. Is this really happening behind the closed doors of my parent's room? Do they just say I love you to each other then be mean to one another? I didn't get the love concept at all.

Needless to say I was devastated with the break-up. I wanted revenge!

I set out to make him jealous because all I really wanted was for him to be my friend and to like me again. After being embarrassed and humiliated I couldn't admit to that fact that I still liked him a lot so I came up with a jealous plan.

I couldn't use just anyone to make my beau jealous. I had to target an older guy. One of the neighborhood hangouts had a smorgasbord of guys to choose from. Finally, I chose one after careful consideration. He worked and had several flashy muscle cars. He had a lot of friends and maintained the typical "bad boy" image. He smoked, drank and got high. He was everything that I knew I shouldn't associate with. However the whole scheme had to draw attention if the scheme was going to win my puppy-love back.

I watched other girls about my age that had older boyfriends and simply just mimicked what they did. It didn't take long for "my target" to take the bait.

However I didn't anticipate the trouble it would cause me to become an actor in the play I had staged. Very quickly and clearly I was in over my head with lying and defiance. My grades dropped in school and I lost the tittles that I held. Then I had the ultimate loss, which was the respect, and pride my parents had in me. I had created such a façade within myself that I didn't even recognize the stranger that occupied my body. Furthermore, my thoughts stayed in a jumble of confusion and my heart was in turmoil.

From time to time I was still being stalked by my uncle and every time I would express my fear and concerns to my parents it seemed to only cause more heartache and grief. I had become overwhelmed of living at home. I had turned to my parents for the help that I needed with my uncle and it just made everyone mad. They were already disappointed with me for the trouble I caused with befriending an older guy. I didn't feel safe nowhere and felt like a total failure yet I felt there was nowhere for me to be. I wanted to be someone else and somewhere else. I was convinced that happiness was elsewhere.

The guy I had befriended was moving away to Kentucky and invited me to go away with him and get married. I seen know other solution to my failed chaos and I decided to run away and become a housewife. I secretively packed my clothes and a few books and went to bed as normal to only lay awake knowing if I continued with the charade things were probably going to get worse for me.

The play was for certain out of control and I didn't know how to fix it. I just wanted to get away from everything and everyone.

I sat down and wrote my parents a letter. I told them I loved them very much and didn't want to disappoint them any longer. I explained to them that I felt like I would ease their burdens if I were just gone. I wrote about my constant fear and how overwhelmed I had become with my runaway emotions. I told them of the plot I had created to win my boyfriend back. I shared the shame and guilt I carried for the family break up. I ended the letter with a simple confession that observing their obvious heartache and disappointments was a constant reminder of the nightmares that lived inside of me that I wanted to forget. I signed the letter expressing my love and placed it with my schoolbooks.

The next morning I proceeded with my usual routine of preparing for school knowing I wouldn't be returning to school or home. I was going to start being the grown-up that people told me to be. I left the house in tears that morning and headed towards the bus stop. However I was intercepted by the one I recently chose to call my boyfriend.

We went to a local restaurant to bide some time so we could return to the house to pick up my belongings. The entire time we were there I was sadden by the thought of what I was about to do wasn't the right thing. Henceforth, the other side of my thought process was telling me I had come too far to turn back. My mind stayed focused on an image I had placed between the two confusing thoughts of my "puppy love". He was aware of what was about to take place and I knew he would show up at the last minute to reconcile with me and his kindness and humor would end my nightmare once again.

Rudely my boyfriend disrupted my comforting thoughts with a demand of "hurry-up".

I didn't say anything just responded by sliding out of the booth and followed close behind him as we walked to the car.

We drove to my house in silence and pulled in the gravel driveway hurriedly. "Get your stuff quickly!" he instructed.

I nodded and went inside.

The house was empty and quiet. Mothers lingering perfume freshened the air. I visualized her long dark hair and her perfect smile. She was the prettiest woman I ever saw. I turned towards my dad's desk and could see his mountain of books from the night before and imagined him sitting at his desk steadily writing and reading. His posture never slumped and he was the smartest and most distinguished man I ever knew. I closed my eyes as if I was imprinting the images to memory and sighed with discomfort. I headed to the steps and picked up my little sister's bear that lay nearby nestled on her shoes. She was so perky and lively. I was missing her already. Greeted at the top of the stairs by my brother and his friend, who offered their assistance and encouragement, I rolled back the tears and tossed aside the confusion roaming throughout my thoughts.

I stood on the porch looking around to see if my childhood sweetheart was in sight and he was not.

My brother and I exchanged our good-byes and I left that day in tears and with heartache.

My boyfriend and I headed for the state line. I slept for awhile and woke to the blaring sound of music from the car stereo. There wasn't much conversation between the two of us. He stopped frequently to make phone calls from pay phones and when I would inquire he would just tell me to mind my own business.

We drove for several hours before exiting the highway. We pulled into the drive of what looked like a deserted motel. Unfortunately it wasn't because he went inside to get a room while I waited in the car.

I watched him as he exited the car. Dressing was not exactly what he did best. He wore a holey T-shirt covered by a flannel shirt that had no buttons. Faded jeans stained with motor oil. His long stringy hair flew about freely in the windy air. I wondered for the first time if he ever really bathed and combed his hair. He was completely unattractive and rude at times. I deliberately sought after this dude for refuge! What was I thinking!

He was finally out of sight and I looked around the nearly deserted parking lot and imagined home. It made me teary-eyed and sad.

He got back in the car and I didn't move. I just stayed in my dreamy thoughts but a sadness of reality came over me. I was here with my boyfriend in a rundown motel wishing I were never here. I missed my family but I didn't want to be there either. I just felt like I didn't belong.

He started the car and drove towards the parking spot marked sixty-six. Without saying a word I got out and began to gather some of my belongings. It was late and I was tired. My mind was kicking into overtime and I wanted sleep.

Once everything was brought inside that we were going to need for the night I was instructed to stay in the room and to stay off the phone. I just shrugged in agreement.

Meanwhile, he made calls to people I didn't know and I laid across one of the empty beds. I began to feel the emptiness inside of me emerge from the depth of my soul. The realization of making a mistake with running away was clear to me. I glared at the phone and thought if I only called home I could make everything all right. I reached for the phone and was interceded by a strong force to the back of my head and a verbal reminder that I wasn't to use the phone.

The gruff voice continued, "Calling mommy and daddy are you?" and added a promising threat, "they will find your corpse if you ever try that again." He walked towards the door and turned towards me with a last warning, "you have until morning to grow up. I have business to attend to. You stay inside and clean yourself up." The door shut behind him and I could hear the lock turning then heavy footsteps as he walked away from the building.

I was scared and sat rubbing my head. A knot was forming and it hurt like hell. I was confused with what I exactly I had done to deserve to be disciplined. Although, my fear didn't stop me from being curious of whom the unfamiliar voices outside belonged too. I listened intensely with my ear pressed against the door to hear what they were talking about. I heard a faint voice ask about a shipment. My boyfriend replied to him that it was all here and that the keys were in the ignition. The car doors slammed and the motor roared loudly as someone started it and drove away.

What was going on I thought aloud to myself?

I could hear the sound of heavy footsteps approaching the doorway and dashed off to the bathroom as my boyfriend came back inside the motel room. I heard screeching tire sounds outside and opened the bathroom door to find my boyfriend peeking through the curtains.

"What's wrong? What's going on?" I asked.

"Shut-up and hide somewhere," he shouted.

Two heavy knocks were sounding on the door. I could only see shadows as two big guys pushed their way through the door as my boyfriend opened the door.

"Where are the three missing weapons?" the stranger demanded.

The other guy remained silent but held my boyfriend at gunpoint against the wall. The question was repeated and with a gesture my boyfriend pointed to a duffel bag in the corner.

The dude walked over and rummaged through the bag and pulled out some guns.

He nodded to his partner as indication to let my boyfriend go and said, "Don't ever try anything like this again!"

Slamming the door behind them the two strangers left.

I was scared and stayed hidden under the bed. I could hear my boyfriend stumbling about the room. Everything was silenced.

"You can come out now," he instructed.

"Who were they? What were they looking for?" inquisitively I began asking. My voice was scratchy. My hands were sweaty. My heart pounded. I was scared to death.

He looked at me with a cold stare and began laughing and throwing money in the air. I was confused.

"Grow-up!" he shouted

He waved his hands in mid air and shook his head at me as to say he was disgusted with me.

"I am going to take a shower. Have this place cleaned up before I get out," he demanded.

Once again I flopped on the bed and covered my head as heavy tears fell from my eyes. I cried myself to sleep that night wondering what I got myself into.

Morning seemed to have come earlier than usual as I was awakened by chatter coming from the bathroom. I could only hear occasional words like: cocaine, guns, heroin, money figures and thirty days.

I was so stupid! I didn't have a clue of who I had been referring to as friends.

A cloud of smoke came from the doorway crack and the odor was so strong it gagged me.

The door opened and a couple came out of the bathroom with my boyfriend. I wasn't introduced. They only nodded in recognition of my existence.

"We will be back soon. Be packed and ready to leave when we get back," my boyfriend said to me.

The three of them left and I was alone in the motel room. I watched through the opening in the curtains to ensure they had left. As soon as the car taillights were out of view I immediately ran to make that phone call home that I so desperately wanted to make. My hands shook with fear of getting caught as I quickly dialed the number.

The phone-line was interrupted by an operator asking for the person who had rented the room. In an effort to explain that he was unavailable at that time, she refused me to place the call.

I sat on the floor feeling defeated in the mess I had created to just make someone jealous. I was discovering clarity of a world I didn't know or belong to.

Startled by the door slinging open, my boyfriend and his friends stumbled through the door, laughing and finishing up with their conversation. It was clear that they had been having a good time while I sat cooped up in the motel room alone.

"Hey girl, get this stuff carried to the car," my boyfriend instructed.

I interrupted, "NO!" and hastily continued, "I want to go home! I have changed my mind and don't want to go with you!"

I received a hard slap across the face with a firm no for an answer. My face was burning and started swelling. I hung my head low as I began to load the car.

After the room was emptied of our belongings, the girlfriend of his friend pulled me aside and in a friendly manner warned me to just follow instructions and everything would be alright. Once again we piled in the car and off to a destination that I was still unclear of.

It was still early in the morning and the fog was dense. Traffic was at a bare minimum. We finally exited the highway onto a secondary road and pulled into a gas station. We proceeded down a lightly traveled road that was lined with trees on both sides of the road and gravel roads turning off the main road. The longer we drove the less traffic we passed.

After hours of driving we approached a small country town. We stopped at a small town grocery store that also served as the postal service. I got out stretching my legs and taking in the view. Mountains of trees surrounded us in a misty haze with warm air blowing freely about. Directly across the road was an almond bricked local church with stained glass in all the windows. The birds were chirping and singing in sync with faraway sounds of cow moos and coyote howls. At that very moment I grasped a small amount of unconfused thoughts and just drifted into God's creation.

No words had been directed towards me the whole trip and the female passenger broke the silence and said to me, "over there," as she pointed behind the church, "is where you guys will be staying. That's where we live and until you guys find a place to live y'all will be living with us."

I just listened and then nodded with approval.

"Come on and I will show you the place while they check on the mail and pick up a few things," she said.

Oddly enough she was friendly to me when we were alone together. She gave me a complete tour of the house and then we waited on the steps for the boys to pull up in the car.

It wasn't long before the guys pulled up and snapped out instructions to unload the car as they headed down a path that led to a barn behind the house. I was puzzled mostly by the gunnysacks they carried on their shoulders. What could be in them I wondered? However, I knew better not to ask questions about what they were doing or the contents of the bag.

Once the car was unpacked the small-framed girl escorted me to a bedroom. The room was dark, felt cold and was dreary. A mattress lay on the floor with a blanket folded at the end of it. A dim light from the next room outlined our shadows on the naked dark blue walls. My mind visualized my family and home. My mom worked hard to maintain a cheery home for us. I sat down curled up in a ball and held my face in my hands as tears ran down my face. My heart yearned for the life I left behind.

My tears stopped at the sound of a slamming door and voices muttering unclear words from the next room. I was drying my tears away from my face as footsteps came closer towards the closed door of the bedroom.

The door opened and in the doorway stood my boyfriend demanding that I find my birth certificate and announcing to me we would be getting married the next morning.

I flipped through some papers and finally found it. "Why do you want this?" I asked as I handed the document to him.

In a mumbling reply, he said, "You will see."

I lay back on the bed and slept until late that evening.

Sleepy-eyed, I stumbled into the next room that was filled with a cloud of smoke and the
aroma of marijuana floated in the air. I glanced around the room and saw my boyfriend sitting at a table with drawing pencils. He motioned for me and I made my way through the crowd towards him.

There were so many people in the house you had barely room to walk. Strange men were making provocative comments and gestures that I managed to ignore as I kept my eyes focused on my boyfriend.

One voice stood out of the crowd as he yelled out to me, "Hey sweet young thing!"

I scanned the crowded room to discover the echoing voice belonged to an old grey bearded man. He was sloppy drunk and loud with crude remarks.

"Hey sweetie come over here and sit on my lap and give me some sugar," he smirked.

I lost focus on my boyfriend at that very moment and I couldn't see anyone else around with the exception of that scruffy bearded man. My body filled with rage and it was as if I transformed into someone else. I grabbed up a beer bottle as I stormed towards him with the bloody vision of beating him. I screamed out "I will beat you! I will beat you!"

Suddenly I felt a gentle hand pulling at my arm. It was the young girl that had befriended me and opened her home to my boyfriend and me. In a calm voice she reminded me to keep a low quiet profile. Her soft-spoken voice calmed me and I gave her assurance that I would do better. We exchanged hugs and I calmed down. The hissing and horrific laughter quieted and I went on into the adjacent room to sit with my boyfriend.

"I am scared," I told him as I pulled out a chair to sit down.

"There is no need to be a baby," he snapped.

He slid my birth certificate in front of me and instructed me to study it carefully and to practice writing the numbers on the blank sheets. It made no sense to me. However, I did as I was told. After a great deal of practice, I managed to duplicate my birth record.

The words "do as you're told" echoed in my head. I was bound by guilt and shame, and

lead by fear. These were the only thoughts I had on a daily basis and at times I just didn't want to wake from my sleep. Home at this point seemed so far away.

A longhaired man approached me as I sat at the table sketching out documents. (You couldn't even see the flaws in the sketching!) He looked steadily at my practice sheets and kept mumbling under his breath. I paid no attention to him and just stayed focus. Then he motioned for my boyfriend. They stepped away together and were engaged in what seemed to be an intense conversation that only lasted for a quick moment and ended with a handshake and a pat on the back. It was obvious they had made some kind of deal.

My boyfriend came back over to the table and handed me an envelope of birth records, photo identification cards and other legal documents.

"Fix these. Follow the individual instructions for each document. There are instructions attached," he said bluntly.

"Isn't this illegal?" I asked.

"Only if you get caught sweetie," he answered.

I worked quickly and managed to keep a steady-hand and after about five hours I had completed the stack that contained driver's license, house deeds, school records, birth certificates and other important legal documents.

Tired and exhausted I found my boyfriend and gave them to him.

"Here is my completed assignment as you requested," I said in a rude manner.

"Go wait for me at the dining table while I make a phone call," he replied while flipping through the stack of papers.

I stumbled across the room to the dim-lit dining room and flopped into the high-back chair where I sat and just waited. My mind wondered off to my world I once lived and knew, and the reality came back to me: now I live in a world of deceit among criminals who were engaged in selling drugs and weapons, altering documents, car thieves and probably more that I didn't know. My thoughts were interrupted by the long-haired man sitting down at the table across from me. He had the stack of papers and was flipping through them slowly and finally slid them into a large envelope and laid them off to the side. He moved to the chair beside me and patted me on the head as he sat down. I cringed at his uninvited touch. I couldn't stand it when a man touched me unexpectedly.

"A job well done sweetie," he said in a friendly voice. "I will bring you more on Friday," he continued. Then he reached into his pocket and handed me a thick envelope.

"Wow!" I shouted as I fumbled through the large amount of money he had given to me.

He reached into his pocket, saying, "Here is an extra two hundred for a bonus. You deserve it." He stood up and gathered the envelopes off the table.

"Don't forget I will be by on Friday and you will have a week to complete each envelope."

I remained still and quiet until the man was out of complete view. Then I couldn't resist taking another peek in the money envelope. I had never seen that much money before. Suddenly the envelope was snatched out of my hands by my boyfriend and he took claims of it by stuffing it into his pocket.

"Thanks. Now go and waitress the card game in the party room." He always talked so nice to me when other people were around and only barked rude orders at me when it was just him and me. He was my boyfriend and soon to become my husband. The only clear sane thought I had was: what have I done?

"I am tired and want to go to bed. If we are getting married in the morning, can't I at least take a nap first?" I asked.

He drew back to hit me and I ducked out of the way and just headed to the downstairs party. I knew there was no need to try to refuse a direct order. After all he only wanted me to fix some sandwiches and drinks for the card players. But when I opened the door I discovered differently. I was expected to strip and perform private nude dances for the winner of each hand. My heart raced with fear of what would happen to me if I disobeyed, but the shame had overpowered me as I imagined myself performing in the nude. I just couldn't do it and I sneaked a bottle of wine and ducked out the patio door. Most of the people were stoned or drunk and I figured that I wouldn't be missed.

Wow, Kentucky is going to be my home, I thought and then just giggled the idea away.

It was a cool night with the brightness from the moon lighting up the sky as if it were mid-day. It was so quiet. The crickets chattered in sync and the sound was comforting. How simple it must be to be living in the woods as one of God's creations. I had become a complex kid living in an adult world and uncertain with life offerings. I leaned against a tree and began to wail like a baby as I slid to the ground. I didn't try to stop the tears from coming or even try to dry my face once they did. I just allowed nature to embrace me with security and comfort for I felt alone and despaired. I drank the first swallow and savored its sweetness and with each following taste I dreamt of being home.

I thought of being that little girl sitting in front of the mirror wanting a friend and now my heart longed for such an opportunity. I thought of the devastation of how my parents must have felt. After all I traded their kindness for a world of evil. I recanted all the mixed emotions that I encountered from the traumatic events with my uncle and the tension it had caused within my family. It all stayed so freshly implanted in my mind. Nothing seemed to take it away. Not to mention the dramatic event that I got myself into with this idiot I was calling a boyfriend and about to call husband after tomorrow. I took another gulping swallow of wine and a sighing breath. Then my thoughts drifted to my special childhood sweetheart. He was the only pleasantness I had and he didn't want to be around me that made it clear in my mindset that I was useless to anyone. Consequently, sadness overtook me and the loneliness within hugged me tighter. I didn't want to think or feel anything more from that moment on and I drank myself into a classic stupor once again until I was numb from my own nightmare.

Startled by a husky voice cursing me profoundly, I was scared to move so I sat still and remained quiet. In a quick swoop the man that professed to love me grabbed me up and smacked me back down on the ground. What was the point of that I remember thinking. I was already sitting on the ground.

Once again, I was in a total confusion of the meaning of love. My uncle loved me yet he sexually assaulted me. My aunt loved me but did nothing to help me. My parents loved me but was ashamed of me. My friend loved me but didn't want to be around me. My grandparents loved me and called me names. My boyfriend states the same word and hits on me and even calls me the same harsh names my grandparents used. I truly felt unloved at that given time because I believed that love wasn't to be of none of what I had been subjected too.

"Where have you been? I been looking everywhere for you," my boyfriend said.

My boyfriend grabbed me back up again and hurriedly guided me to the car. I was unsteady on my feet due to the alcohol consumption so he yanked me off my feet and carried me the rest of the way. Once we got to the car he bent down and opened the car door and threw me in the backseat like a useless rag doll.

"We are going to Virginia to get married and you better start minding or you will get worse," he warned and added,' did you hear me?"

I never answered; I just nodded in agreement and laid down on the car seat.

*Niveah Jewell*

We drove all night through the mountains on dark deserted roads that seemed to never have an ending but yet didn't seem to go anywhere specific. Is that what my life destiny could be compared to is a mountain deserted road? I just closed my eyes and cried in silence. My whole being within agonized in turmoil but didn't make complete sense to me.

Daylight began to break through as I awoke from a drunken sleep. I wiped my eyes and fluffed my hair with my fingers. I straightened my blouse and smoothed out my jeans. I gave myself a look-over and I looked the best that I could with considering the accommodations.

"Good morning," I whispered.

"Should be since you slept all night," he replied.

I knew not to give an answer back so I just rearranged myself in my seat and stared out the window. Finally a road sign was visible and a town was just minutes away.

My boyfriend pulled up in front of a small red bricked building. The sign that stood out front of the entrance read "Common Pleas Court."

"Is this where we're getting married?" I asked.

"Yes it is sweetie. Do you have any objection?" he replied.

"No, this will be fine," I mumbled.

# Chapter Three

THE SMELL OF PINE drifted through the air of the Virginian Mountains. The sky was filled with fluffy clouds as if it were heaven's bed waiting to cuddle up its prospects for rest. The morning dew was thick and offered a shivering dampness. The early morning sunrise was peeking through to promise that the day would soon begin. The town shops that lined the streets were still closed as owners began to move about slowly to have them ready for their customer's. Pigeons gathered on the iron rod benches that sat outside each shop door. The welcome of the small quaint town was a warm welcome of stay as long as you like.

We sat in silence inside the car waiting for the courthouse to open. I knew it to be useless to try to strike up conversation so I only daydreamed of a perfect prince. I knew that getting married today wasn't the right thing to do but on the other hand what else was I suppose to do after I had already said ok. It was going to be better after we were married I thought.

The new day began as we exited the car and walked up the long narrow sidewalk. He held my hand as we walked and even smiled. My thought was right. Things were going to be different. I gave a blushing smile back at him.

My boyfriend reached to open the heavy glass door for me and with a polite voice added, "After my lady."

The entrance was deep dark wooded that had a dreary weariness about it. The walls displayed black and white photo framed pictures of the town's years of progression. The hard wood floor squeaked as we walked towards a gray-haired lady that sat behind the enclosed glassed window at the information desk.

"We are here to get married," I announced.

"Do you have identification cards and birth records?" she asked without looking up.

"Yes ma'am I do," I answered as I slid the documents under the glass.

She reviewed the documents without conversing and gathered more papers together from a file drawer.

"Here, fill these out," she said.

We stood before a hallway desk and steadily began to fill out the papers.

I went to turn in the packet to the woman at the window and stood quietly while she reviewed them.

"How old are you dear?" she asked me.

"Sixteen," I answered. Knowing I was lying, I wondered if she knew. I was getting nervous that she was going to find the alterations. Then what would I do?

Sign here at the "x", she instructed.

I was relieved. She didn't suspect anything.

We signed and handed them back to her.

"Go wait in front of "room one" and someone will be right with you," she advised.

We walked down the hall holding hands and it was a clear thought-- everything was going to change and be good from now on.

We stopped in front of room one and the bailiff was already waiting and the judge was prepared to perform the ceremony.

"Are you here Miss of your own freewill to marry this man?" the judge asked.

My mind raced with a dozen thoughts but they all led to don't do this.

Hesitantly, I answered, "Yes Sir, I am."

Feeling as though I were a stolen hostage from chaotic trauma and forced into bondage, I wanted to scream "Help Me", but instead I just smiled with innocence and repeated, "Yes Sir".

I do's was exchanged and abruptly we left through the exit door.

My newly wedded husband stopped me in route to the car and said, "You now belong to me and don't let me have to remind you." Although the words of warning were harsh those were the last kind words he spoke to me.

We drove back across the state line through the mountains towards our hide-a-way. I felt very uneasy of nothing specific but only knew something bad was about to happen. Oh dear God, what have I done, was the only rational thought I had.

The only words spoken were by my husband and I listened with no questions or comments. He spoke of how the police were looking for him. He talked in detail of drug and weapon trafficking and the trips he'd made frequently to southern Florida. He warned me to be on my best behavior and rambled on about rules that I was to follow. The main emphasis was that I was not leave the house and never to use the telephone. I was to talk to only the two people that he already had introduced me to. I sat motionless and his words began to fade away with my own thoughts. I felt trapped in a lion's den about to be devoured. I only intended to make my sweetheart jealous and it has led me to a fake marriage, illegal activity and running away. I was inside a world with no way out and at times it appeared as if I was looking through a window of someone else's life.

I just wanted to be numb. I didn't want to feel any kind of emotion. I just wanted to belong however I felt I didn't belong in my family's lives and I definitely didn't belong in this world of explicit crime. Where did I belong at the young age of fourteen? I wanted to be in a drunken stupor where I created a happy place.

I broke the silence by asking if we could stop for a bottle of wine to celebrate. I pointed out a billboard that had an arrow pointing to the left for the next gas and grocery store. He agreed with no argument and slowed down to prepare for the turn-off.

"Would you like anything in particular?" he asked.

"No, just something really sweet," I answered.

It was a relief to have him out of the car. I was free to chatter to myself aloud and sometimes I would find things to laugh about when I was alone. It was the time I felt safest. However, this time I spent trying to breathe and digest all the details I had been given. I was scared and confused. I suppose this is what his idea of me growing up was and if it were I was certain I didn't want to.

He returned to the car with the wine I had asked for and some beer for himself and a bag full of snack food. I removed the cap off a bottle of apple wine and drank myself to sleep.

I woke up just before we entered our hideout town only to find darkness had came while I slept. We pulled up in front of a rundown shack that looked deserted and condemned.

"Get out!" he shouted at me. "This is where we will live." He exited the car as if he were in a hurry and slammed the door.

I got out slowly as I wiped my sleepy-eyed face. I walked slowly towards the open door. I stood in the doorway looking around at an empty large room that housed a coal stove. To my right was a doorway covered with a sheet and behind it was a bedroom. Straight ahead through the living room was the kitchen. The moonlight coming through the windows cast shadows throughout the dark shack but the despair of gloom filled the rooms as I glanced around once more. It gave a harsh feeling of dreariness. With a cold shiver I cringed at the thought that the old run down shack was suppose to be my home sweet home. It was a lonely home just as I was lonely for a home.

My husband went outside to talk to his friends and I took a deep swallow and rolled back the tears from view. My jumbled thoughts came together to ask myself how this all could be real. How did a fake boyfriend become a fake husband? What had I done? What am I going to do?

# Chapter Four

THE SCREEN DOOR SLAMMED shut as my husband came into the house. Without saying a word and with a single gesture he motioned me to the bedroom.

Holding back the privacy curtain that was intended for the usage of a door I stood in the doorway and glanced at the bed and dresser that filled up the room so tightly that movement was limited. I just wanted to cry.

"Where will you be sleeping?" I asked.

"Here with you! Are you that stupid?" he snickered at me.

Abruptly he pushed me across the lumpy bed. I laid still and just looked up at him.

He continued, "As my wife you will have sex with me when I tell you to and this being our wedding night we will start now." He paused and stepped backwards to remove his clothes and turned and said clearly to me, "You will do as you're told so get undressed."

He left the bedroom and I could hear him in the next room mumbling words in thin air and the sound of papers being scuffled through. I sat frozen, as if I was a statue, in the middle of the bed. The curtain flung open and he sprung towards me screaming words that made no sense to me. He smacked me in the face and I lost my balance and fell to my side. Instantly he grabbed my feet and turned me towards him as he ripped my clothing from my body. He then stood to the side of the bed and finished removing his clothes and I only laid still in my terror.

He straddled my body and pinned me down as he climbed on top of me. I was terrified. I screamed! I kicked! I needed to free myself and I couldn't. I had lost the battle. He forced my knees apart with his leg as his hands kept my shoulders tightly held against the mattress. I cried in pain. He had his way with me and then lifted my head to him by the back of my hair and kissed me on the mouth.

He began to laugh aloud, "Get used to it. You are my wife now."

I cried sobbingly. This wasn't what I had imagined a wedding night to be like. I was relentlessly scared. I cried some more.

He sat on the side of the bed and smoked a cigarette and then turned to me demanding food.

I slid out of the bed from the opposite side and put my clothes back on. The buttons from my shirt were gone and my zipper to my jeans had been broken. I replayed the incident that just had taken place a few minutes beforehand and silently cried to God to help me.

"Bitch, get used to making love. That's what grown-ups and married people do," he smirked as I headed to the kitchen to make his dinner.

I felt nasty and ashamed. I wanted to take a bath desperately.

I stumbled to the kitchen. Every step I took was instant pain inside my groin and down my legs. Bruises had started to appear on my shoulders and arms. My face was swelling with burning pain. My tears wouldn't stop flowing. I want to be gone from here but to where was my focused thought.

I had never cooked before and remained clueless of what to do as I stood in the middle of the kitchen floor. I slid under the kitchen table and buried my face in my hands as I hid myself in my fear and confusion.

Suddenly, I heard footsteps stomping with every step and quickly getting closer. I hurriedly attempted to crawl from out under the table and instantly I felt a blow to my chest and fell backwards on the floor. He, my loving husband, had just kicked me in the chest and knocked the wind out of me. He continuously kept kicking me as I crawled around the floor trying to get away from him and screaming for help. It was a pointless cry for help that no one ever heard.

His screaming words were only an echo of sound. In my desperation I couldn't clearly hear him and all I could hear was single words like bitch, fix, listen and whore. I stayed focused on getting myself to a safe location.

He finally stopped kicking me and I curled up in agony in the corner of the kitchen floor. My thought was clearly to myself of why I just wouldn't listen. My parents only asked that I listen and forget and I wouldn't leave well enough alone. Here I am now and my husband is just asking for me to listen and obey and I can't get it right either. I collapsed on the floor in pain and in tears. I felt a crushing weight on my back as he stepped on me to leave the kitchen.

"Bitch you better get up and get my food cooked if you don't want a real beating," he said. His footsteps went away.

I pulled myself to my feet and hobbled to the refrigerator to get out some hamburger. I managed to get back to the counter by the stove and pat out two patties. I turned the burner on low and kept flipping them until I thought they were done. I proceeded with the simple task of placing them on buns with all the condiments available. I placed them on a plate with a fake pleasant smile and took the dinner plate of food to my husband.

I hurriedly walked away back to the kitchen where I started to clean up the mess.

Startled by a commotion of screaming directed towards me and stomping feet approaching my direction once again I began to slide up against the wall as if I could blend in with it.

"Bitch you can't do nothing right," he said.

Just as my face become one with the plate and food dripping down my face, he continued yelling and scolding me.

"You eat this shit if you think it's so fit for me to eat," he commanded as he broke the plate against my face. The impact shattered the glass plate in my face and all over the floor.

"I am sorry and I will do better. I promise I will," I pleaded.

Months passed and I tried to mimic everything I had seen my own mother doing around the house. Unfortunately it didn't save me from what had become a daily beating.

Six months had passed. I hadn't talked to anyone nor had I seen anyone with the exception of my husband. When he would leave the house I would sit in front of the window and imagine the sunshine on my small framed body for I had been forbidden to go outdoors even with him present. He would leave everyday and padlock the door from the outside to ensure that I wouldn't leave the house. Most of the time it was a blessing because I felt safer alone and would pass the time by listening to the radio and telling stories aloud to myself. Sometimes I would just sit by the window and daydream of being somewhere playing in the sun and laughing. Other times I would visualize a tall dark handsome man that would come and take me from the horrific challenge of life.

The reality of my life had become horrific. Everything I did was wrong from cooking to cleaning and especially the sex area. There were always significant punishments besides the beatings. For instance, withholding my food for days at a time was one punishment. Learning experiences as, my husband preferred to refer to them was to watch other females perform sex with him. I came to believe my life was traumatizing because I wouldn't be obedient and as a result I would just make my spouse angry. Home was so far away in my thoughts that I could hardly grasp them at times for my parents would be very displeased with me now was the image I embedded when I thought of them and my siblings. Although I missed them and longed for them, I knew I couldn't be with them.

One early summer afternoon I walked outside carrying two glasses of iced tea. I wanted to surprise my husband and his friend with something cool to drink since the sun was at an extreme peak. I had only been outside twice and it was now mid-July and I wanted to savor the outdoors as well as do a good deed although I knew that the cost was going to be an extra daily beating.

Quickly unappreciative of the gesture I was told to get back in the house. The footsteps that followed me were a very familiar heavy sound and as I pushed open the door he shoved me inside. He tore my clothes from my body as he yelled accusations of me flirting with his friend. When I was fully exposed he began punching me and beating me. In his outraged, stoned state of mind, he beat me until I lay helplessly on the floor. Just as I thought the punishment was going to end he would start all over again hitting me and kicking me. At some point he stormed off outside. I could hear him screaming names at me through the open door and a car door open and closed. I was almost in an unconscious state and couldn't focus clearly due to my face swelling. But I clearly heard the front door slam and was aware of his presence once again. I was scared and couldn't move. The pain was excruciating and the only screams I could make were deep inside me as I was unable to bellow out. He dragged me across the rugged wooden floor and I could feel the wet blood pour from my back and legs. He whipped me with leather straps that day until my body was raw and bled like the flowing river of tears within my soul. He gathered me up and I lay limp in his arms as he kissed my forehead just before he tossed me to the floor and I landed in front of that old coal stove. I lay helpless in my blood and with difficulty breathing I agonized in pain. He walked over to me and stood beside me calm and still. Raised his foot across my stomach and stomped the breath from me. I thought it was my last breath that I would take. He knelt down at my side and propped my head against his leg and mumbled a few words of his love towards me and that I was going to have to learn to be a wife.

I closed my eyes the rest of the way in relief that this wasn't the day I would die. My mind carried me to a field of colorful wildflowers where I was laughing and running. I was free! I always could find comfort in my mind's imagination.

There wasn't a place throughout my body that wasn't in pain. I dare not move as it would only be torment. My thoughts raced through my brain with questions in search of answers. How could I endure much more? People didn't live this way. Where was my rainbow? A brighter day would come.

A vicious blow to my abdomen and a horrific laugh interrupted my restoring comfort mode. As I opened my eyes there stood my husband over me in laughter while he smoked a cigarette. He just shook his head and bent down and kissed my swollen face. I felt like nothing at that point.

He turned to exit the house and I wanted to scream out 'never come back' but the words wouldn't come from my mouth. I lay still waiting for the sound of the padlock like I had many times before. That always meant he would be gone for days which gave me time to heal. All I needed was to hear that last fumbling click of the lock and the car door slam and that would be all the confirmation I needed to cry out in torment and know I would be safe. I cried myself to sleep lying on the cold wooden floor while I lay naked in my own blood.

Awakened by a scratching sound at the door I crawled to the window to see what it was. I agonized in pain all the way there but I was frightened and wanted to ease my fear by knowing what was on the other side of the door. To my amazement it was a stray dog. I crawled and scooted to the door as if I was going to let him inside but instead I curled up next to the door pretending I was lying next to the whimpering lost dog. I imagined I was stroking his fur and rubbing his belly as he licked me with his gratitude. I named him Charlie and began to tell him of my secrets that were hidden behind the barricaded door. I felt at ease with my newly found dog Charlie and drifted back off to sleep.

When I woke up I could barely see out of either eye due to the trauma and swelling. I touched my face gently and felt the cuts and swelling covering over my entire face. I glanced over my naked body and could notice I was almost one gigantic bruise. I lightly touched my stomach and ribs for they hurt the worst but I couldn't withstand even the lightest touch. I had severe pain with every breath I tried to take. I had been beaten severely this time and I turned to my side and hugged myself as tears rolled down my face. I was in pain and needed help and there was no one.

Eventually I scooted one inch at a time towards the sofa in hopes that once I made it there I would be able to pull myself to my feet. It seemed so far away from me and I stopped and had to rest in between slow tormenting movements. I made it! Each time I made it through my torture of hell I strangely felt a sense of accomplishment. I managed to make it to the couch and pull myself up on it and I stretched out and fell fast asleep.

I wakened unsure of what day it was but it was obvious that I had been asleep for days. The swelling had begun to decrease and some bruised areas had started turning a dingy color. I vaguely remembered the horrifying ordeal but it became clearer and an instant replay when I stared at the dried up blood on the floor. I was still in severe pain and had trouble maintaining a steady cycle of breathing. I stood and walked extremely slow to the kitchen sink where I managed to wash up.

Taking the same pathway back through the living room I made it to the bedroom. I was cold and wanted some warm clothes to put on. I was unable to put anything over my body so I settled for a tattered robe. I hobbled over to the bed and lied down. I was out of breath and tired from just trying to make it this far. I lied down and in a silent thought I gave recognition to my family as I once again fell into a light sleep.

I slept until late that evening and woke feeling rested. I heard the scratch of my dog Charlie at the door and walked to the door slowly but I smiled all the way there. He brought me excitement and comfort when I was in need and a sense of purpose as my voice eased his whining.

Three days passed and I had begun to regain some strength and started to feel better. I cleaned on the floor until the violent scene was just a memory. My soreness got a workout and once again I felt like I had accomplished something—the survival of living life another day.

I still remained confused of how many days passed by but I had a feeling that it wouldn't be long until my husband arrived back home.

Early in the evening of the following day I heard the familiar sound of an engine roar and knew the monster was back. There were routine sounds of the car doors opening and closing. However this time there were unfamiliar voices mixed in with all the other familiar voices. I braced myself for the strangers that would be coming inside shortly and rehearsed conversations that would not prolong a conversation. Then that sound of the padlock being removed was a definite sign that everyone's presence would be visible soon. Swiftly the hell gates were opened and there I was scared but in the same sense was pleased that I would see someone's face. I yearned for human contact at times. I recognized one of the men as being ,Chuck, the man I was intimidated into making documents for but the rest of the people I had never seen before.

The scruffy man approached me immediately with a job proposal that I could begin right away. It was very simple. All I had to do was take cars to people that had made a purchase and I got paid for doing so.

After I had agreed to take the job, I noticed my husband looking awkwardly at me. I walked over to him and told him that I was glad he was back and asked if I could have the job.

"Yea, I guess you can do that for Chuck for awhile." He paused and stepped closer to me and placed his hands at my waist. I felt uncomfortable and didn't know what to expect. "I love you," he said and simply walked away.

I never answered. I only took a deep breath and sighed with relief that

I was not smacked or ridiculed. Maybe he even meant the words he had spoken. It wouldn't have mattered to me at that point. I had only one agenda and that was to make it back home alive someday. Besides, love, what the hell did that mean anyway? Love seemed to me that it only gave others permission to be cruel to you and maybe that's why we hardly ever used the words in our house growing up.

The man that my husband referred to as Chuck came over to me with another young girl following close behind him and handed me a set of keys and instructions to where to leave the car. Sound simple enough and really all I had to do was follow behind the girl to a parking lot and leave the car I was driving and ride back with her. When we got back to the house just about everyone had left with the exception of the two guys that were waiting for us to return. Upon our arrival I was given an envelope that contained $1,500.00. I was excited needless to say. My husband took half and the rest was mine.

I had made over $20,000.00 in delivering cars in just a few weeks. I also picked up some document alterations as well and I had a lot of money stashed away for that special day I could leave would eventually come.

My husband's road trips were less and less but nothing had changed. He still said I was a lousy wife and late at night after his company would leave he would beat me for it. I had grown to have a high tolerance of pain and would endure each blow with an odd sense of pride. I tried to avoid him as much as possible.

Once a week I was permitted to have my partner in crime stay and socialize for a couple of hours after we had made our deliveries. The work was plentiful and the money was plentiful and I had a bonus…a friend.

One Friday night she and I returned to my house to find my spouse waiting on the porch with her boyfriend. They had been getting high and drinking and announced they were going out of town when the morning sun came up. Our good-byes were exchanged and my husband and I walked into the house together.

I looked into his eyes and saw a distinctive distant glare. He kissed my forehead and told me he loved me and bellowed out in a horrific laugh. I was always to expect the worse when I would hear that laugh and it would terrify me.

"I know you do," I said as I walked to the bedroom. I changed into my night clothes and grabbed a book to read as I lied down on the bed. I hoped if I stayed out of sight he would forget about me.

I heard a car pull up later and my husband went outside to visit with his friends. They were partying harder than usual so I just stayed put as to avoid any confrontations with my spouse. I was scared and offered myself reassurance that just maybe my daily beating would be overlooked and forgotten.

They finally moved the party inside and I could hear the laughter and jumbled words being mistaken as conversation. Sounded as if they were all having a terrific time and that only meant it wasn't going to end anytime soon.

I laid my book down and thought about what other couples might have been doing. I didn't know what love was but I was for certain it wasn't the torment I had to endure. My thoughts were interrupted by cruel laughter and extreme loud conversation by the group of guys and girls from the next room. What was about to happen?

The wonder of what was to come next was always with great apprehension and left my insides in a bundle of fear and anger. I learned to expect the unexpected at any given time. Surviving until the next day had become a daily task. The noise from the next room became louder and louder as the intoxicating folks partied more and more. My eyes began to grow heavier as the night progressed into the midnight hours but somehow I wasn't at ease and restless. I knew that the evil would soon take place but when?

At some point I had fallen asleep and was awakened by a knee striking my groin. Ouch! My body trembled in pain as I screamed out. My hands were collected together above my head and tied with a rope. I was being dragged off the bed with strands of my hair. What was happening? Was this real? Squirming and kicking I tried to break free from the grasping hold but once again I failed and was dragged across the same floor that I had bled on just weeks ago. His group of friends sat around laughing and gawking. A few slaps here and there I knew I better stay still or else the ultimate price of death would eventually be paid.

My husband yelled to one of his boys, "Throw me those straps from behind the couch!"

Meanwhile my husband found the opportunity to express his love for me and proceeded to let me know I was his everything in life and he kissed my forehead and then my lips. I was more fearful of him at that point that I froze and allowed numbness to enter my whole being inside and out.

I asked, "What are you going to do to me?"

"It is time for you to have another lesson on being a wife." He laughed as he reached for the leather straps.

I begged and pleaded with him to let me go but he only yanked me to my feet and threw my frail body against the coal stove. His knee slammed into my groin and he grinded his knee into my pelvis to hold me still. The pain was excruciating and I screamed aloud and begged the spectators to make him stop. It was as if no one heard and in some gross manner they were enjoying "the show" and finding pleasure in my torment. He began to bind me to the stove with the straps one at a time. Once he had me secure he took a knife and cut down the middle of my silky gown. I was exposed for view in my bra and panties hanging by the stove. The humiliation filled the pit of my stomach and I could only scream in agony. The tears fell like a tidal wave and the display only made for laughter for the room of people that stood by. My husband leaned forward and kissed my lips hard and once again I heard the echo of I love you. He stepped back and lurked at me with a smile of accomplishment. He bellowed out into a grotesque laughter and I spit in his face.

I looked down towards the floor in shame as the reality of my body plastered for viewing came to full circle in my mind. I was devastated, helpless, ashamed, embarrassed, and most of all, alone.

My husband stepped back towards me and pulled his knife out once more. He walked towards me grinning and stroking the blade of the knife with his fingertips.

I screamed out, "Cut my throat, please. Cut my throat, please. Just let me die."

"Help me! Someone please help me!" I cried in agony.

No one stepped forward to my rescue. However, my husband now stood before me and quickly took his knife straight down the middle of my body and released my privacy for full view.

The men made several crude remarks and sexual gestures as they continued with their card game as if nothing weird was going on.

I continued crying out for help and each time I got no response.

My husband would pass by me and smack or hit me with a closed fist somewhere on my body. The restraints tightened around my body the more I would make a simple movement. My skin was being torn apart for I felt a burning sensation and a warm stream of blood running down my body where the straps had been placed. My body ached and the pain was becoming unbearable. My stomach was queasy from the thought that these sick minds found this ordeal to be amusing.

The lights were dimmed and the music was turned up a notch or two. The female visitors began to take their clothes off. The girls started to kiss and fondle each other. One by one the men had sexual encounters with the females.

I was grossed by the ordeal and closed my eyes as if I weren't there.

My husband noticed and smacked my face while making demands that I open my eyes.

He stripped down naked in front of me and leaned forward to kiss my forehead. Professed his love for me and turned towards the girls and the three of them began performing sexual favors for each other. At one point my spouse blew me a kiss and reminded me to watch and learn. Finally the sexual fantasy orgy was over.

My spouse instructed everyone to leave the house and to wait outside. He then walked over to me and stroked my hair from my face and as he did he gently held my face in his hands. I was scared and had no idea what to expect next. I only knew that my body was feeling rigid and my mind was at a destitute state.

He took a couple of steps backwards and just stared at me.

"You stupid bitch, did you learn anything?" he asked.

My husband began to undo his belt and whip me with it. I cried loudly in pain and only hung my head as to admit that I had been defeated.

"I should light this here stove and let you burn!" he said to me.

He continued whipping my naked body while the blood trickled down my legs and beating my face with his closed fist until my eyes swelled to a blur.

"I ought to burn you!" he kept repeating. He would stop and hesitate while lighting a match as if he were going to light the old coal stove. My body trembled in helplessness and I begged and pleaded at his mercy.

The bleeding from the restraints and the whipping had caused my raw skin to burn like fire. My arms and shoulders were in piercing pain from being strapped behind me. My legs were numb from the inability to be able to bend. My face swelling and my body bleeding I just wanted him to finally end it all.

"Just go ahead and kill me you bastard!" I screamed aloud through my tears of sorrow.

Suddenly, he stopped and stared. I could see a crooked smile form across his face through my blurry vision. He only blew me a kiss and spoke the evil words I love you to me. Then he staggered towards the door.

"Untie me please! Let me loose!" I begged loudly.

I heard only the sound of a chuckle and the door closed. The padlock was being fumbled with so I knew I would be attached to the stove for the next several days.

The salty tears ran down my face and my heart opened up to pour out all the heavy regrets I had stored in my soul. I knew earlier that evening that I was going to be beaten and tormented beyond recognition but death was a reality check when I realized I could die. My body suffered in piercing agony as I hung by the leather restraints and my soul screamed in silent terror as I grew too weak to form words from my lips.

In my mind I played the horrific scene over and over again. Eventually I was able to gain control and stop the visual replay and drift into my wildflower field of serenity. I was running and jumping. My long chocolate brown hair flowed through the wind. I held bright red balloons that floated high above my head. I was free, peaceful and most of all safe.

My peaceful thoughts were interrupted by a sound of a car engine, the slamming of car doors then the padlock unlocking. It had only been hours since he had left me there. What was he returning so soon for? Is he coming to finish me off? Did he forget something? What was my evil husband doing? The front door slung open wide and there in the flesh I was on display for my husband and all his friends to gawk at as they once again entered the house of "secret horror."

The men and women passed by me and stared with strange questioning eyes and added giggles of disbelief that the display of me was real. I could plainly hear the chatter among the group with the bizarre snickering. What did she do? He would never do that to me. Look! You can see her bones. She is bleeding all over. The words of their observations only echoed like in a theater horror moving being played.

I dropped my head in shame and hid my tears deep inside me.

"Help me," I muttered aloud.

"Let me go and I will kill myself a lot faster than this!" I pleaded.

My tears began to surface and I begged once again for someone to kindly help me.

People only passed by me on their way to the kitchen as if I weren't there. They sat around smoking weed, drinking alcohol, injecting heroin and snorting cocaine. I had been wrong about the party and orgy being over it had just began. The stereo blared "ACDC" as the girls danced around the room provocatively and some had started taking their clothes off while others just made out.

Some guy walked up close to me and whispered, "I am going to touch you." The smell of alcohol and stale cigarette smoke covered his body and breath. The man stunk! He lifted my head as his eyes glared over my nakedness. His words were slurred but he managed to speak them aloud to me only to repeat: "I am going to touch you." He forcibly began to fondle over my bleeding, numb and agonizing body.

The thought of him touching me made my skin crawl. With the same eeriness as it had done when my uncle touched me and when my husband did as well. I was scared and filled with rage. No sounds would form in my throat. I was helpless one more time at the hands of evil.

I felt so many emotions going through me and my life reel began to play. I was bound and terrified. I was fourteen and too young to die.

Once again hours passed and the moonlit sky had brightened the dim overcrowded room. Through one swollen eye I could tell that people had started to leave. My body just hurt and the emptiness subsided deep in my soul. I had no one. I knew no one. When would my prince come? Would he come too late?

My husband stumbled towards me. He untied my hands and arms. They fell to my side limp and numb. Then my abdomen was released followed by the chest restraint. I choked on the first breath I took. My chest felt as if I was going through a wind tunnel. I was unable to breathe deeply with the straps around me but now it felt like I couldn't breathe at all. The pain in my chest was excruciating with every breath I took. I dropped to the floor as my spouse removed the last restraint from around my knees. My body was weak and felt mangled as he kicked me and demanded I get up and walk.

I couldn't feel most of my body and it tingled as it would when a limb would fall asleep. Dried and fresh blood covered my entire naked body. I attempted to stand but failed. The pain was too harsh and I had no strength in me. I scooted on my side and was making little by little headway to escape my horror.

"OW! Please don't hurt me anymore today." I begged with a faint whimper.

He didn't listen to my crying plea and only continued to kick me in the groin and the back as I scooted my way to victory.

"You are useless! I don't know why I keep you around!" were the barking words he had for me. "I should trade you in," he concluded.

"Please do." I managed to scream out.

"I wish you would," I added.

I received a disagreeing comment with a kick in the stomach and a fist of blows to my face.

With little strength left I inhaled a deep breath and forced myself to ignore the pain and focused on getting to the next room. With all my might I got to all fours and crawled on my hands and knees to the bedroom. I collapsed on the floor at the end of the bed and could only feel a single tingle throughout my entire body. I knew I was hurt badly but it did no good to voice that concern.

I sobbed so hard that my breath was taken away. The laughter from the next room seemed so far away. I reached for a sheet that hung from the bed and I tugged at it until my exposure you could no longer be seen. I snuggled against the wall and listened to the fading sound of "I love you" being said from my husband.

Love, I thought to myself, that I can live without.

My face was swelling and tears burned like fire through my opened flesh. My whole being was suffering. A compelling silent rage settled inside of me as I mumbled softly, "I will not be defeated." I drifted off to sleep as I heard the padlock shut to enclose me in.

Awakened days later I stood to my feet and stared in the mirror but only could shake my head in shame. My eyes barely could see through the swelling. I had been beaten black and blue until knotted bruises surfaced all over my small framed body. Dried scattered trails of blood covered my entire body and at a glimpse the sight that stared back from the mirror was more than I could bear.

I thought of my family and my heart poured out the stored tears. I turned my thoughts to my beau. It was a happy generating memory that refueled my energy and strength. I cried out to God in selfishness of defiance. I screamed, ranted and raved to my reflection until I began to feel some relief.

I was angry with everyone and even God. I was lonely but believed that there was no purpose for people in general in my life. They didn't help you. They only laughed and ridiculed and took advantage of you. I had no use for that longing. I heard countless of times that people were good, the world was evil but that life was good. It made no sense to me now; I knew different. The fact was I was fourteen and alone in a world of nothing but cruelty. The people were useless in this world I was in and I was uncertain of how I felt about the ones I left behind. God, where was He actually? Love, I didn't want any part of. I had saved nearly $150,000 and the first chance that I got I was getting out. I wasn't scared but overtaken with raging thoughts of revenge and survival. My reflection didn't resemble the little golden curled hair girl who used to sit and play with me when I was sad. I stood be forth the mirror as a stranger to even myself.

Weeks passed by and my body was healing. I was alone and at some level found a small amount of peace. I went about the house freely singing my tunes that I would create. I found pleasurable entertainment dancing about with my broomstick as if it were my dance partner and my so ever loving prince. When evening came I would sit with my journal and write stories and thoughts until my dog Charlie would come scratching at the door. Then I would go to him and talk to him through the closed door and listen for his soothing sigh of relief and I would know he was fast asleep. That old dog loved me and never once seen me or felt my hugs for him. I loved him too. It always felt safe being alone and on lock down and in some kind of unnatural way felt non-confining. I had no worries of being demeaned for that period and could take moments to be me.

I combed my long wavy hair and could feel every knot on my head and began recalling that last treacherous night that I had seen my husband. Tears filled my eyes with sadness to only remind myself that I was a pretty girl and one day I would have my fairytale.

I sat and talked with my stuffed animals and made believe they were my friends. They held all my secrets. They were the closest I had to human contact on a daily basis.

Although I couldn't talk to my parents and siblings, I would write to them. I would write them and tell of horseback riding, sharing recipes, picnicking and singing in the church choir for they were all the things I would have been doing had I not been held hostage in hell with the evil gate keeper.

The food was rationed to me as a behavior modification so therefore I learned to really take an accurate inventory and continue the rationing for myself. My daily intake would consist of five crackers with a half of a hotdog or twenty-five macaroni and cheese noodles. I stayed weak most of the time and nauseated. My stomach and throat would sometimes hurt from just swallowing food which at times would also keep me from eating.

A sudden sound from outside interrupted my comfort mode and the gruff voice was shooing my dog away. The familiar sound of the padlock was being removed. Instantly my body trembled in fear as the door opened to reveal my evil caretaker {my husband} holding grocery bags.

"These are my groceries. Get these put away and get your grocery bag from the car." He commanded as he walked through the house.

I felt like a dog must have felt when he would get bones and scrapes thrown to him.

Henceforth, I was grateful and obeyed immediately. I got his things put away and headed out the front door to fetch my food rations.

I could feel the fresh air. It was magical. The sunshine was warm but the brightness irritated my eyes. I was soothed for the moment with a glimpse of normality. The freedom of that feeling ran through my being like a rippling creek. I just smiled and reassured myself that I was going to be okay. I picked up the bag and went inside.

I put the few items away and went to wait in the living room for my scolding explanation of the results of his inspection. It was all such a routine. He would beat me and leave. He would return after several days and inspect the house for signs of something which I never asked what they specifically were; followed up by a list of demands that I always completed promptly. Lastly I would walk around over the following day's wondering and trying to prevent the next beating or punishment. It was insane. It was sick. I had to find a way out.

He finished his inspection and sat down in the chair across from me with a dark cold stare. I remained calm. I didn't know what to expect because something was different and I didn't have time to ask questions. The details were speaking for themselves and it was clear something was going to happen.

Leaning towards me he asked, "Who has been here, bitch?"

I attempted to explain that there was no way anyone could have gotten in or out due to the padlock.

Abruptly he leaped towards me and grabbed me up and flung me like a Frisbee across the room. I didn't weigh much and my ribs were visible so every time I landed on them the pain was excruciating. My husband kicked and beat me until I no longer could move. After several hours of enduring the physical pain he inflicted on me, I thought my life would be over before morning could rise.

He picked my lifeless body up and carried me to the car. He laid me gently on the backseat. My husband kissed my forehead and whispered to me, "I love you."

I was unable to move and I lay completely motionless and only heard myself murmur "Where are you taking me to?"

He responded with a hysterical cruel sounding laugh, "Time to trade you in."

He drove for what seemed to be hours and finally the car came to a complete stop. He got out and opened the car door and I could only see moonlit shadows in the darkness. He stood outside the door exposing his genitals and then pulling my pants off to expose myself to him, he climbed on top of me and had is way with me. I screamed in agonizing torture within for I had no ability or strength to make a sound or to fight him off. Once again I had been defeated and at the mercy of evil. My husband raised his body weight off me and bent over and finished removing my clothing. My body lay openly exposed on the back seat in desperate wonder of what was to come next.

He grabbed my feet and pulled me halfway out of the car and stopped to inform me that I was nothing and I leave with nothing. He roughly cradled my face in his hands to kiss me and once again he told me he loved me. Then proceeded to finish pulling me from the car by my ankles and violently threw me in a nearby ditch. I heard the car door slam shut and felt the pebbles hit me as the spinning tires sped off.

I lied in the ditch in torment. I cried uncontrollably. I was scared. The pain went throughout my entire body but my mind felt relief in knowing I was finally freed from my torture chamber. I was lifeless in my shame, regret, humiliation and embarrassment. I could hardly breathe and every small breath I took I felt like I was taking my last. My legs felt a tingle all the way to my hips; my arms would only bend halfway. My blurry eyes were dimming as the swelling to my face was closing them. The tears kept flowing in anguish and relief.

Sounds of the coyotes howling in the far off distance and an occasional vehicle passing were keeping my mind relieved that I could still hear and therefore I wasn't dying yet. My image of the wildflower field comforted me as my imagination led me to snuggle with the image of my dog Charlie. A sense of freedom gathered my strength as I attempted to move my limp body to a crawling position. I had to prepare myself for getting help. It took all the energy I had to get my head above the ditch but I did and I just propped myself against the ground and waited.

I kept dozing in and out of consciousness but I held on for with every ounce of strength and hope of being found. I had to survive the wait.

I could hear the sound of a semi engine roaring in the distance. I knew I had to get the driver's attention. I thought to myself this may be my only chance at getting help. I crawled to my knees and held on with one arm while I forced my broken arm to wave in the air as a distraction. The truck's headlights blinded me and I whispered helplessly, "Please God let him stop to help me."

I saw the taillights come to a standstill just a few feet away from where I laid. From pain and exhaustion my body fell limp and I slipped further back into the depths of the ditch. "Please God help him to find me."

I heard the stranger yelling, "My name is Charles and I stopped to help. I won't hurt you. Where are you Miss?"

I forced out the words that were struggling to surface, "I am here; please help me."

He came running towards the sound of my voice and shined a flashlight down on me. He bent over me and took off the jacket he was wearing and wrapped my nakedness inside of its warmth. He hurriedly carried me to his truck and laid me across the seat. The kind stranger reached above my head and pulled down a blanket and wrapped me up tightly.

# Chapter Five

THE DRIVER PLACED THE roaring semi into gear and off to safety we headed. I felt so relieved I finally had been rescued from the hands of one of Satan's angels.

"Miss who done this to you? Who left you here to die?" he asked.

"My husband," I responded in a whimpered voice.

"The closest hospital is over an hour away but I will get you there," the stranger promised.

I laid in peaceful agony at the mercy of a stranger as he drove to the hospital emergency room where I was to be treated. I could barely focus. My breathing was shallow and body was numb.

I could hear him on the "CB radio" telling the emergency room staff that he had found a young girl that had been beaten and possibly raped and was bringing her in. It was me that he was speaking of and his kindness aroused a joyful tear that I was finally to be freed from the insanity life of torment that I was growing accustomed too as being a normalcy.

I was immediately seen and multi testing was done. The hospital social worker came in and brought me clothing. She was a very nice lady and had foreseen that I would have difficulty in dressing myself so she offered her assistance. She then instructed me to sit back on the bed comfortably so that she and I could talk.

"What has happened to you, my dear child?" she asked.

I told her of the past two years' occurrences. She didn't interrupt but only let me talk. She listened with amazement and sometimes disbelief looks would show in her facial expressions. The woman only listened and asked no questions and offered no solutions. Once, she broke in and told me that there were a lot of healed old fractures that had showed up in the x-rays.

Finally the woman stood and walked behind her chair. She stood still and shook her head while intensely taking a deep breath. Then she blurted out, "You're going to have a baby." Another sigh she took and added, "The doctor will come in and speak with you further. Will you please give us your name, age, and tell us how to get in touch with your parents."

The social worker paced the room and then took her place back in her chair across from me. We sat and glared at each other for a brief moment. The thoughts that went through my head were all so overwhelming and I had already given so much detail. I rationalized my identity once again. I really had no worse trouble that I could get into. Defiance and secrets had already taken me to the pits of hell. I was rescued for help so I should take it.

I broke the silence with a simple fact that I feared: "I am fifteen and too young to die." Thoughts ran ramped through my mind. If I returned to my husband the result would be death. However, if I were to return to my parent's home they would be devastated and outraged. All I could offer were tears and they poured out simultaneously like ocean waves.

The doctor entered and offered me a Kleenex as he took a seat beside me and the social worker. He flipped through the papers that he held in his hand and tossed them aside.

"Miss," he began, "you are extremely young and I am not sure how much more abuse your body can withstand."

I only listened with my head held down in shame. I stared at each individual glossy white square floor tile through teary blurred eyes. I felt hopeless and lost. I only listened quietly to everything I didn't want to hear: the truth of the facts.

He took a deep sigh and began to reveal his findings: "You have a dislocated shoulder, two broken wrists, severe abdomen and pelvic bruising, multi facial fractures, fractured ankle, two fractured ribs, not to mention the multiple open wounds and trauma to your eye. The x-rays also indicate that you have had several untreated fractures that have healed. Miss you are now eight weeks pregnant."

He stood and paced the room. I sat and cried. The social worker sat quietly.

"Let us help you!" he concluded.

With a face covered in tears I nodded in acceptance. I revealed my name and age followed by names and numbers to get in touch with my family. I talked several hours with the police and the hospital staff.

I was escorted to a small isolated room and given some food. Then I lay on the couch and slept for hours.

I was awakened by mother's soft caring voice.

My parents cuddled me at the bedside with a gentle loving manner.

Once again the police arrived shortly after my parent's arrival and I had to repeat my story one more time. Only this time I included outstanding warrants for my husband from other states. Dispatched was notified and an immediate arrest was made.

I felt relieved and safe. My heavy burdens had been lifted from my heart with simple truth. Help had been received and love reunited. The marriage was annulled due to illegal technicalities. I turned state's evidence and no charges were filed against me in return for my cooperation of testimony.

I returned to my hometown in Ohio with my parents. I was emotionally unprepared for the realization that my parent's had moved on with their lives and for all the changes that had occurred during my absence away from home.

"We will make room for you in your sister's room," my mother said caringly.

"Okay," I replied hesitantly.

It was as if I had lost my place in existence with the family. No one spoke of my absentee and that's all I could think about. Unfortunately I wasn't permitted to speak of the events. However, the events haunted me while I was awake and kept me from falling asleep at night and when I did sleep, I was only having sleepless nightmares. For each day that passed, the guilt, disappointment, anguish and heartache that I caused became overbearing. I just wanted to scream! The presence in my parents' home was only a constant reminder of my inadequacies and I no longer felt as if I belonged. I was on eggshells making sure that I perfected everything once again. I felt awkward and confused. I felt extreme loneliness with nowhere to turn.

I remembered distinctively the last time I had these feelings that I went to my parents and revealed 'my secret' it had caused devastating family feud. I for certain did not want to relive that ordeal so I remained quiet and stayed to myself alone in my room. I became isolated in my own shame and guilt. My insides were overloaded with emptiness. I needed a friend, someone I could download with but who do I trust? I became over self-conscience with what I said or did. I existed in my own prison again due to the secrets that I bared alone. The only difference in the violent cell I was rescued from and the one I entered at home was this one was perfected and I had already failed immensely to measure up. I needed something I could identify with and feel safe and of sound mind.

December quickly came and my baby girl was born and I was overwhelmed by a new fear. Motherhood.

The hours of pain were exhausting. The confusion of delivering a baby was frightful. I was confused most of the time of what to do but the nature's course didn't stop and eventually the pain ceased and I was handed the ultimate gift at Christmas: a precious life of a baby girl. Her chubby cheeks almost hid her deep blue eyes. The softness of her skin was soothing. I had delight contentment with just gazing at her. I had a different kind of tear that day: tears of joy!

Four days later my mother picked us up at discharge. It was Christmas Eve. The snowy day was filled with a brutal cold but held for me a new warm beginning. My heart was at peace with love for a bundle of treasure. The love in my heart was embedded with excitement and fear and wrapped with a loose ribbon of nervousness.

Upon arrival home mother escorted the baby and me inside. The rest of the family was waiting impatiently to exit for the annual Christmas dinner at grandma's house.

Immediately when the house was empty the realization of the truth of being on my own was now the reality. The entire time that I was pregnant I was reminded of how I was a grown-up. Followed by instruction that I was to be responsible, accountable, and selfless and become a provider. Henceforth, I was clueless how to really define and accomplish most of what was being preached to me yet I knew deep within that I had to do it. I was fifteen and a grown-up.

The winter had been harsh and now spring was turning to summer quickly. I had worked the summer doing odd chores for neighbors that consisted of lawn care, gardening and the ultimate baby-sitting. I also had acquired a job at a small local nursing home as a nurse's aide. I worked and saved all my earnings with the exception of buying the baby's needs. I had developed a plan and it was working. My thoughts were far and few of my life before. The more I busied myself the further the memories seemed to drift.

That summer I got a car and an affordable apartment. I learned how to pay bills very quickly and developed a sensible routine. Among all my uncertainties I knew one thing for sure: I could not fail. My life was confusing of where I belonged; I did what all adults did which was go to work, pay bills, clean, cook and take care of a child but wasn't welcomed into their world. Moreover, I had too many obligations to mingle with people my age and besides I had already been alienated from most of them anyway. I was isolated once again in my own creation. I drank a lot to manage my own grief and confusion. Then I drank more to keep from being scared. I didn't eat much due to running low on money and food but mostly I developed a frame of mind that I could never be fat. My once slender athletic built had become a wrinkle scar of a woman's body that I detested. I felt as if I was the only one that belonged with me. Everyone witnessed success as to what they saw visibly; however, I was dying inside with emotional turmoil.

The familiarity of loneliness kept me in imagination of dreaming and hoping of that one day my dreams would all be true. The reality was that I was a child with hopes and dreams but I had a huge interruption. Most days I didn't want to greet but it was my love for my baby girl that kept me trudging through each day and gave me a smile when I just couldn't. My sadness dwelt as a festering sore deep below the surface of the naked eye.

Two years passed by and the man I had ran off with and married illegally was due to be paroled. I began to have horrible flashbacks, nightmares and paranoia of him coming after me. I would imagine him lurking around corners just waiting for me needless to say I knew first hand of his capabilities and was frightened. My images began to feel so real to me that I became panic driven so I moved another forty miles away to a new apartment and found a better paying job. Paranoia still ruled my thoughts and actions.

Months went by and I finally found a way that I could relax beneath my own flesh. I developed typical days that involved mostly work, window shopping and the park. The favorite part of the day was winding down playing in the park with my rambunctious toddler. We would play until we both were worn to a frazzle and then walk the shortest path to our humble home. She would always pick flowers from yards that we would pass by and in broken words tell me she loved me from here to there as she held out the flowers to give to me and reached out her tiny arms for me to carry her. She was the love of my life.

One early spring evening I gave my little girl a quick wash-up and put her to bed right after dinner in hopes to just sit down and regroup from an exhausting day. I piddled about picking up toys and cleaning the bathroom while she fell asleep. When I knew for sure she was sound asleep I headed downstairs excitedly to watch some uninterrupted television. However, I became alarmed halfway down the steps when I noticed a curtain blowing from an opened window. Everything seemed quiet and safe from the stairwell so I continued cautiously the rest of the way down the steps. I headed directly to the open window and closed it and double checked the locks.

"How could I have been so careless," I scolded myself aloud.

I ran around the house checking the doors, windows and touching all the locks twice just to make certain we were locked in safely. I opened the closet doors and the pantry door to ensure that no one was in the house. Just as I reached for the last closet door handle I was interrupted by a whimper coming from upstairs from my baby girl. Paranoid, I panicked and I ran up the stairs as quickly as I could, taking the steps two at a time. I found her fast asleep turning over in her sleep. She must have been dreaming for she smiled as I tucked her in tight with her blanket.

I took a moment and stared down at her. The moonlight outlined her chubby cheeks. Her breath was soothing as she drifted further in her dream. The crooked grin she held on face reminded me she was happy baby.

I whispered, "I love my girl", bending over the crib to leave her with a gentle kiss. I continued in quiet voice, "I will always protect my baby girl. You are my pride and joy."

I released a relieving sigh in my gut and turned towards the door. I looked back over my shoulder one more time before I headed downstairs to ensure she was sound asleep.

Startled by a rattling sound from somewhere downstairs my heart began to pound as if it were going to jump out at me. My mind raced a mile a minute. What could it be? I locked everything up and double checked it all. I heard a disturbing noise again. I knew I had to get down the steps but my feet wouldn't budge. I was frozen in my fear. I made a mental reminder that I had to go see what it was and that it probably wasn't anything. I took a deep breath and down the steps I went. Slowly and cautiously I reached the bottom step and paused as my eyes glanced through the darkness for a safety check. I decided it was safe and walked over to the light switch, and as I reached to turn it on someone grabbed my arm and slung me to the floor.

"You were a bad girl to think you could ever leave me," the gruff voice spoke in the darkness.

The man that once beat me senseless now stood over me in my very own living room. He fell to his knees over top me and pinned me against the tiled floor. I squirmed with all my might to break his hold on me but his weight held me securely. He pulled out tape and succeeded with taping my mouth closed. His knees held my arms still against the floor. I continued in rage squirming and kicking with the lower half of my body. He laughed aloud in a crude horrific manner that I had once often heard.

He began to pull my head off the floor repeatedly by using the back of my hair and just for kicks he would punch me in the face. I continued trying to fight him off but he overpowered me with his bodyweight. He leaned back on his knees holding my head tightly in his hands and began pounding my head on the floor and telling me how useless I was. The fear in me was silent and his eyes stared at me coldly. I didn't know what to expect and my body was beginning to throb with pain as the blood dripped warmly from my face to the floor.

Something shiny was reflecting in the dimness of the unlit room. My memory quickly recollected the knife he once used to cut my clothes from my body and here he was about to do the same thing. He ran the sharp blade under my shirt against my skin and bellowed out that I was his whore and bitch. He kept repeating other words only my mind wouldn't allow me to process the thoughts. With a single sudden flip up the wrist he cut my top down the middle and exposed my breast in full view. Then he took the knife and held it at my throat and clearly said, "I don't know why I just don't slit your throat."

I held completely still in fear that he was going to kill me. My mind drifted to my precious girl. I could only think of what would happen to her if she were to wake up and I said a silent prayer that God keep her sleeping in her dreams. Then my eyes formed heavy tears of sadness of what would await her if I were to die at the hands of this maniac that fathered her. My prayer continued silently asking God to not let me die tonight.

Reality came back to me. His body laid heavy over me. His eyes were glassy and bulging and drool oozed from his lips. He was an evil man yet I was able to withstand and overcome the fear as I regained a clear mental awareness and I began fighting him off again.

He only sat stiff over top of me laughing and ran that cold sharp knife blade up and down my exposed body. He cut open my jeans to view my lower body and rubbed the knife blade against forbidden areas of my nakedness. Then he proceeded to expose himself to me.

I closed my eyes to shelter my pain as this evil man raped me. My mind retrieved the safety of the wildflower fields where I mentally remained while the bastard had his way with me.

Abruptly he stood to his feet over me and began kicking me in the sides and stomping me in the chest until I was breathing shallow breaths. Every breath I took started to feel as if it were going to be my last one. The silent screams of terror lay behind the tape and once again I was helpless at the hands of evil.

He finally stopped beating on me and sat down on the floor next to my exposed bleeding and bruising body. He lit a cigarette and kissed my cheek.

"Why do you make me be mean to you?" he asked in slurred words.

Everything was a silent coldness and darkness. I lay still in agonizing pain. My eyes were swollen. My face bled. My private parts bled. The rest of my body felt broken into pieces and excruciating pain ran through my entire body.

He stood while he finished his last puff off his cigarette and stomped it out on my stomach. He abruptly turned to the front door and exited quickly and I heard nothing except the sound of a slamming door.

I reached for the tape across my mouth and yanked it off. I cried tears uncontrollably. I felt overwhelmed with shame and defeat. My body felt nasty with filth. I pulled myself to my feet and struggled up the steps. With every ounce of breath I had left and every ounce of energy I had in me I made it to the top. First I went to my sleeping child and faintly whispered a profession of my love and a promise to keep her safe. Then I went to the shower and scrubbed the filth from my body several times. I couldn't get clean. It seemed as if I as dirty inside of me all the way to the bones. I stood under the water crying and terrified. The hot water ran out and the coldness from the showerhead tormented my flesh. I got out and dabbed my body dry with a soft terrycloth towel.

"Will a thousand and thousand's of showers ever be enough to wash away the filth of a man?" I muttered aloud to the silent bare walls.

I stood at the doorway of my baby girl's room and just held my head down as if somehow I had failed her. I have got to get him away from us I thought.

I hobbled back downstairs and made a phone call to the police. I sat at the kitchen table and waited for their arrival.

The tears and agonizing pain haunted me with fear but I only waited.

They finally came and I told the story of the intruder. I wanted to file charges. However, after I explained the identity of the assailant, the cards changed.

"Miss, get a restraining order until he cools off. This is a simple domestic matter," the officer stated.

Within a few days of that horrifying incident I moved to another apartment across town. Once again everything was seemingly okay to those from afar. But I knew this evil man would be back one day and that I needed to be ready for him. I had no one to help me. My family believed that I exaggerated the conflicts between the once known as husband and the police just tossed my complaints aside as domestic disputes. I feared for my life and my child's life and had only myself to depend on. I took defense classes, exercised regularly, and mastered in target shooting. I would be ready for the next encounter even to the point of vigilante law.

I walked through the house several times before we left each time securing locks windows and doors and upon returning repeated the same inspection trail to be assured no one had entered. My little one slept with me at night. We were residing in a prison instead of a home. I intensely feared for the safety of both our lives.

I had put that tragic night aside in my mind and moved forward with my life by making safety the number one priority. Then I developed a routine of work and playtime. Everyone imagined everything was okay and I too believed it would be since I stayed prepared and confident for the next face-to-face with evil and cruelty.

Not long after my twentieth birthday I was introduced to a real nice guy. He was in the military and home visiting with family. We exchanged numbers and corresponded a lot. We hit it off wonderfully. I hid the fact of all my past drama and he treated me as if I were normal. I mostly liked the fact that I finally had a grown up to talk to and spend time with occasionally. Work was going well for me and I would rush home to get domestic chores done so I could spend the evening on the phone talking to my dude. The one thing he always wanted to talk about was childhood memories and high school experiences. I dodged those conversations like the plague since mine was obviously not the experiences that another could relate to. Mostly the shame of the truth often haunted me and so I began to create my own version of the truth until it seemed almost real. We established a nice safe fantasy romance by mail and phone. I had a realistic belief that nothing would ever become of us and therefore I was doing no one any harm.

A couple of months passed by and I found out I was pregnant. I was devastated. I counted back days and menstrual cycles and it was the night of the rape that I had conceived the child I was carrying. I had pushed the rape out of mind and gave it a label as nonexistent. Consequently, an innocent unborn child was to drudge the occurrence back to life and haunt me. I cried and screamed vengeance for women that had ever been at that man's hand of violence or of any other man's. Then I became depressed and suicidal. Where do I go and what do I do?

I had never spoken of that horrible night with anyone except to the police and they by no means believed me so I decided to keep quiet. I needed someone to talk to and to guide me with options. I wrestled with ideas of abortion and adoption for weeks but the clock was ticking for a decision to be made. I needed my parents. I was scared to death to contact them over this ordeal since they had firmly told me long back that my life's messes were my responsibility to clean up. I finally swallowed my pride and put aside my fear and went to them.

I told of the tragic that had occurred after my house had been invaded by the unwelcome intruder and the result of the rape had conceived a child. They listened with no questions and interruptions. I finished wiping my tears and held my head up and looked anxiously at my parents waiting for reassuring words.

The advisement I received after laying out the issues at hand was simple and bold. "You're to have the baby. You have no right to give up what was part of us or you!"

Their response rang through my ears that made me feel as I had done something wrong. I went for a long drive that evening and just thought silently. I played back events all the way to childhood and for once my accomplishments were starting to outweigh my failures. My life was becoming uncomplicated and now I had to deal with the issue of the rape along with a new baby. I was devastated as I left their house discouraged and hurt.

When I arrived home I listened to the answering machine. There was a message I played that was an offer from my parents to raise the child as their own. I simply listened to it a couple of times and already in such an emotional turmoil state I only flopped on the couch and fell asleep exhausted.

I awakened early the next morning with one single thought: I got to get back into the fight again! There weren't time for me to gravel in my grief and sorrow for a baby was arriving in just a few months.

The remainder seven months had gone by quickly and even upon delivery I was uncertain that I could take care of another child.

Soon after the baby and I came home from the hospital I had gotten us on a daily schedule. I went back to work. I still had my phone friend that I looked forward to everyday but I kept the baby a well-hidden secret from him. I just didn't want to answer any questions and certainly didn't want ridicule or judgment.

One late night a hard steady knock sounded at the front door. The treacherous man that had tortured me for several years of my life now stood in the dimness of the porch light knocking at my door. I watched him secretively pacing back and forth in a staggering sway wondering if I should call for help. I concluded that the police didn't help the last time and that they were probably not going to this time either.

I took the babies to their room and got my gun. I hurried back to the staircase and sat at the top of them to collect my thoughts and energy. I knew eventually that he would kill me even if no one else believed me. I couldn't leave my girls in this world without me. He continued to knock harder and started hollering. An eerie silence fell and I heard footsteps. He had gotten inside. I met him halfway down the winding stairwell with a 32 staring at him. He became fixated on the gun pointing at him and said some words that I didn't process. I blocked out the sound of his voice and his threatening actions completely out of my system and remained calm. I backed him down the staircase steady and slow. The silence grew thick and cold as tension filled the atmosphere.

"You don't have the guts, bitch!" he bellowed out.

"Leave me alone!" I shouted.

Then I began reminding him aloud in a calm cool collective manner of all my haunting memories: "You beat me endlessly, nearly starved me, broke my bones, raped me, humiliated me, cursed me, and kept me prisoner." I smirked at him and continued, "You still think I don't have the guts?"

"I love you!" he professed.

It was silent and tense as we exchanged eye-to-eye contact.

"You will come away with me," he demanded.

"I'm not going anywhere with you and want you to go away and leave us alone." I responded.

I took a deep breath and continued, "Take this as your only warning. I want you out of my life!"

He stepped towards me and I fired one shot. I had shot him in the knee and he fell to the floor. This time it was him that begged for his life and not to be hurt. I actually heard him say once again he loved me. With no acknowledgement of the words spoken, I was the one that laughed as I drug him down the steps and out the door to his parked car.

I drove him to the hospital emergency room. I parked away from the entrance door. I turned towards him and studied his agonizing face that was obviously in pain. I couldn't help but wonder if he felt the same pain that he had caused me over the years. I took a deep sigh and proceeded to get out of the car and walked around to open his door. I dragged him to the sidewalk and left him there. I stood over him with a cold blank stare. I warned him if our paths were ever to cross again that I would kill him the next time. I walked away quickly and didn't look back.

I felt some kind of sense of relief as I ran back to my apartment. Upon arrival I cleaned up the dried blood thoroughly and then stood over my babies in comfort of knowing that we would be free from the haunting from then on.

I sat on the couch and processed what I had just done and knew it would be just a matter of time before I would be arrested.

The police came that afternoon and arrested me for the shooting. I was released that evening on an $50,000 bond pending a court hearing. Early that morning when I arrived back home I sat and pondered on the thought of going to prison for protecting my babies and myself fron the evil cruelty of one man. After all the police and my family refused to believe the truth and left me with little choices on defense. I couldn't fathom the idea of not being with my girl's.

Then I recalled the image of the new man in my life and his marriage proposal. I went and looked at my babies as they slept peacefully in their own beds. They were so precious and innocent. They certainly deserved the right to have a father. Tears ran uncontrollably down my face as I picked up the phone to accept the marriage proposal.

He was excited and shouted cheerfully. I cried with confusion and listened to him ramble on about what a wonderful life we were going to have.

I hung up the phone after a few minutes and sat down on the floor between the babies' bed and cried. I hid my face in my hands and cried heavily. I didn't want to move away and marry this guy, however my girls needed me and I needed them. I rationalized their need for a daddy and my boyfriend was good to them and would make a good dad for the two of them. I concluded that I had done the right thing by them and laid my head to rest.

# Chapter Six

I ENJOYED IMMENSELY SHOPPING for a dress and preparing for the event. However, something kept nudging at me that this wasn't the right decision for me. I would confide in others the concern's that I had and was convinced by others that it was only "the jitter's" and not to worry so I went on with the plan. We were married and moved to the islands of Hawaii to begin our life together. The sound of his voice telling me I would learn to love him kept in my mind as if it were a nagging itch.

"All you have to do My Love is remain faithful, cook, clean and take care of the kids the rest would fall into place." was the words he had spoken to me and passively with obedience I agreed that I could do all that.

The first weeks into our marriage I questioned my decision to marry a man I hardly knew and move thousands of miles away from anyone I knew. First of all I find out that he had spent all of our money and was trying to get a loan for an apartment. Secondly, I discovered the town homes he described to me weren't even built. Lastly, I found pictures of him and an exotic blonde celebrating our engagement on the beach. His only response was, "I will make it up to you."

Trust him--no I didn't. Believe in him--no I didn't. Feel safe with him physically, yes, but trusting him with my emotional well being--no I didn't. I would confide in him and he would only use the information to hold over me during an argument but it was more important to me that I never be physically hurt again. I would just have to find a way to deal with hurt feelings and a blemished ego and that I did by drinking heavily.

Our marriage went on for several years with him cheating. Although at times I could almost understand why he did because I had such a difficult time giving my body to him. He mostly liked performing sex to me while I was sleeping without my knowledge or acceptance and that would make me feel violated and raped all over again. I began to see him just like the other men from my past and I didn't want to be with him but in a sick twisted analysis he treated me better than anyone else and he was a good father.

I buried myself in my children and made them my complete wholesome heart and now there were four of them. I would witness their enthusiasm in their daddy and somehow I found comfort and love in that very act.

I had become accustomed to being alone and so I found no need in seeking companionship from my husband and sex I could do without. I rarely needed to talk anyway. So I decided that my life was good and I accepted the marriage just for what it was: safety, security and mostly a family for my children.

I kept my secrets of my prior life hidden deep within. He never asked so I never felt like I was lying. The only thing he ever asked about was the girls' father and I told him I had been violated and it never came up again. As time progressed I had to reveal some situations that were abuse related since I woke out of nightmares in a rage or excessive sweating. I had to give reasonable explanations. However, being truthful later brought me to the most frightening times of my life. Several concurrent events took place which included divorce, homelessness and jail time. However, my outlook on life took a change for the better.

One early morning in February of 1987, I got out of bed, showered and dressed and preceded with the early morning chores which consisted also of getting the two oldest girls off to school. I stood anxiously on the front porch steps and watched them cross the street to the schoolyard. I remember thinking about how much I loved being a mom. I mumbled secretly in my mind "they were more ready to grow up than I was of letting them."

I hurried back inside the house to throw in the next load of laundry before I started the little ones' breakfast. Just as I had finished preparing bowls of cereal with sliced fruit and buttered toast, I heard the sound of little footsteps moving about upstairs.

I scurried up the stairwell to greet my little babies with morning kisses. While I washed them up and changed diapers I recalled their simple innocence and carved it into my memory. I'd witness something new in their curiosity of adventure and a quirky grin would come over my face. Being a mom was my whole reason of greeting each day. They were sunshine on the gloomiest day and gave my heart a warm smile. We finished washing up for the morning and headed downstairs.

A knock at the door interrupted our busy typical morning routine. I opened the door and was greeted by two M.P.'s. Shadowing off to the side stood my husband with a smirk grin.

The taller M.P. handed me some papers while simultaneously asking, "Please state your name Ma'am."

With great apprehension I gave my name.

I turned my attention to the shorter M.P. In short explanation he had explained that they were there to escort me from the premises and I had five minutes to gather my belongings and surrender my dependent identification card.

In total shock, I stood lifeless, as I grew frustrated and confused. Skimming over the papers that were handed to me I read words like divorce, separation, removal and no re-entry privileges. My body felt cold and numb. I was completely dumb-founded.

I could feel the tugs of my babies at my lower legs. The room seemed to have grown smaller. My mind was racing a mile a minute with no words coming from my lips. My face became flushed with my vision impaired with tears. I stared relentlessly at the papers in my hand. I thought there must be some mistake.

Suddenly I felt a pull at my shoulder and an immediate coldness to my wrist.

The shorter M.P. broke the silence and said, "I need to finish handcuffing you. Please lay the documents aside."

My mind could only speak with no volume. I fought back the tears that were waiting to dump like a summer rain. Heavy.

My mind was ramped with questions and thoughts. How could this be happening?

A loud voice interrupted. "Time-up," the officer stated, "you have been handcuffed for transport. It is standard procedure. You will now be escorted to the Main entrance and will be arrested if you attempt to return to Post. Your dependent privileges have been revoked. May 22$^{nd}$ is your scheduled court date which will be held in the Honolulu Courthouse."

"I understand, sir," I exclaimed, "but there must be some mistake," I looked over at my husband in dismay.

He shook his head at me and replied with a smirk, "I had decided to file for divorce." More words were being said but I couldn't hear them due to the preoccupied thoughts of why a short brunette stood beside him.

I stood motionless and handcuffed as I heard the cries of my babies and I was helpless to their needs. I began to feel anger start to travel through my body like a raging ball of fire. I pulled back away from the officers and they politely warned me that I would go to jail for resistance if I moved again.

I felt completely overpowered by humiliation, embarrassment and helplessness. All the mixture of emotions overwhelmed me with shame and despair. I cried with my head held down and walked with the officers to the police car.

I was placed in the backseat of the car. I looked out the window at my sadden-eyed babies and then gave my husband a cold stare. He returned the look and added a wave as he turned to give the brunette a kiss.

"That Bastard!" I mumbled under my breath.

We drove in silence, which was good because I was about to lose control of my tears and my temper. The only way to maintain control was to remain silent.

Upon approaching the gate entrance, the M.P.'s reminded me of the consequences that would be enforced if I were to return to post premises. They proceeded to get out of the car and opened my door with instructions for me to step out of the vehicle. While I turned to be unhand cuffed, I saw the brunette that had been at my house driving my truck. She deliberately slowed down and waved as she passed by. I flipped her a definite sign of anger; she, with a smile returned the gesture and sped away.

I on the other hand was emotionally distraught with heartache, anger, shame and betrayal as well as embarrassed. I just quickly wanted to get away from the eyes that stared at me. I ran away from the post gate as fast as my feet would carry me.

I could see a public bench in the near distance. With my heart pounding and my legs weakening, I ran harder. As I approached the bench, I slumped over it and let out a scream of terror! With sobbing tears running down my face, I sat down and cried. Finally, I regained my breath and with a sensible composure I stood to walk away with no destination in mind. I just walked around the streets of a nearby town and from time-to-time I would stop and glance in the store windows at their displays. However, my thoughts were centered on this morning's disturbances.

I turned down an off-street and sat down on the sidewalk. I watched the traffic pass by with wonder of where they all were headed. My eye caught a glance of a school bus then immediately I began to panic. Unaware of the time of day, it was obviously time for my girls to come home from school and mommy wouldn't be there to welcome them. I sobbed with heartbreak.

Who would have their snack ready? Who would ask of their day? What about homework? Bath? Stories? Playtime? Questions filled every thought and the only answer was 'not mommy'. I trembled with frustrating fear, sadness, anger and loneliness. My heart hurt and I had nowhere to turn. I cried and felt torment throughout my entire body. My husband had warned me many times in anger that this day would one day come and here it was but I was unprepared.

The reality that I couldn't see my children had come to surface. I felt as if I was coming unraveled like a ball of yarn: one strand at a time.

I stood and began to walk down a long deserted road lined with pineapple groves. My thoughts were jumbled and I was sad and lonely. I felt as if I might as well have been identified as a corpse because I died a little with every revealed reality.

I had nowhere to go but I knew I had to go somewhere. So, I walked. Being led by moonlight, I turned in the direction of the North Shore where I knew of an isolated local beach. I walked alongside of the road kicking up rocks and dirt. From time-to-time I would look back to see how far that I had come. I walked blind sighted with tears most of the time.

Suddenly, I began to hear the sound of the ocean waves crashing, extremely loud. I knew I didn't have much further to go so I began to run towards the sound of the waves. The closer I got to the ocean the cooler the air started to get. Finally I felt the cold water brush against my feet. Instinctively, I fell to my knees screaming out, "God help me! I don't know what to do! I'm lost and confused! Show me God what to do."

I glanced around and nobody was in sight nor was there any sounds being made. With the exception of the sounds from the wild boar from across the ridge, everything was quiet. The sea life splashed about throughout their domain. I twirled in circles of confusion, sobbing and screaming out into the cool air to God.

I spotted a nearby cove with large rock openings. I made my way towards the secluded cove. I fell down and crawled on my knees in between two boulders. I felt the weariness of my body turn into physical pain. I lied completely still.

A night rainfall set in with gusts of cold winds blowing. I propped myself up on a rock that was behind the boulders and closed my eyes. I whispered a prayer and I asked, "God, why?" My mind played the day out in thoughts as I drifted to sleep.

Birds rustling through a nearby trashcan awakened me. The sounds of the cars from afar sounded hurriedly as the driver's sped to their destinations. I watched as couples walked the beach in a happily shared moment. Men with metal detectors savagely combed the beach in search of lost treasures. The morning was a complete scene of the gloom that had settled in my life. I ducked my head back behind the rock as if I was a turtle seeking shelter in the shell. I was scared to stay and yet I was scared to leave with nowhere to go so I curled my body into a tight ball and lied still in my own drowning emptiness. The thought of staying hidden behind the rocks somehow offered a safe refuge.

I fell asleep for a short time and awoke crying of a total realization that I had no home. My heart felt as if it had been torn out.

I sobbed. The tears ran down my face like a hard rain in a thunderstorm. I missed my children. I even missed my husband. I had no clue why he did this to me. I thought we were at least friends. I had agreed that we lived separate lives and I took care of the house and the kids and he tossed me out to be devoured by emptiness. Where did my life go? I was filled with such confusion that I was empty from the inside out.

Later during the day I climbed a cliff-side and sat overlooking the ocean. The water and the sky appeared as if they united as one. Seagulls swooped down and caught their favorite catch of the day. Dolphins jumped at least six feet in the air creating a simple splash. The whales were busy calling for their mate of choice. The whole scene together gave a picture perfect of endearment within nature.

However, I sat pondering over the idea of ending my life. Misery and doom had taken its place within me and I was overwhelmed with a future I couldn't visualize. Quite frankly, at that moment, I just wanted to die.

Intervention of a falling rock startled me. I turned to see an old man making his way towards me. Frightened, I realized I had no way to escape. The closer the gray-haired man got I could hear him hollering, "Little girl, little girl, don't be afraid." As the words were spoken I felt a soothing calmness over my body and within my soul. The fear had subsided.

The old man reached out his hand and said, "I am Charlie and I have come to help you find peace." He sat down near me.

I recalled a pleasant memory of comfort from the unseen dog that I named Charlie and felt the same easement as I did from so long ago when I would need someone at my despaired moments. I cautiously began to relax.

Charlie took out two small bowls of poi from his oversized coat pockets and as he handed me a bowl he said, "Eat." We ate in silence. I couldn't swallow fast enough. I was so hungry. I ate like a vulture attending a fresh kill. Hunger hadn't been one of my thoughts of priorities during the past few weeks.

The old kind man revealed a papaya from another pocket. He began to peel it with a jagged edge knife and shared it with me. It was juicy and quenched my unknowing thirst. I smacked my lips together and quietly murmured a thank you.

A raven gathering the peels that were tossed aside broke the silence. I stared deeply at the black raven's stature. It stood so assured and confident. The deep blue that glittered through the thick layered feathers shined with a brightness of beauty. She looked like she would have spoken with an abundance of gratitude as she flew away. The simple beauty that was bestowed had left an impact on how I wanted to be like her.

Charlie interrupted my admiration of the bird and said gruffly, "Little girl you need some guidance before this world devours you."

Puzzled and uncertain I shifted my body weight to a comfortable position but didn't speak. I listened intensely as Charlie continued, "Look around you and see the appreciation of life that has been given to you."

I glanced around but didn't really notice. However, I was eager to hear what Charlie had to say.

He commanded, "Listen carefully to my words. Admire with gratitude the beauty before you. Then you can survive the unknown with what you do know. Believe in the One who created it all. Trust and you will live." He paused and turned towards me saying, "You have no right to claim anything including your own life. Little girl, it all belongs to God." Charlie lifted his hands to the sky as if he really meant to go even further and bellowed, "God holds the answers and the plans." Once again he looked at me and told me, "Don't attempt to make him your equal by trying to change His plan."

"I have just lost everything sir!"

"My child, to lose is sometimes the gain besides you can never lose what you don't have, missy"

I leaned towards Charlie and cried in his arms as he hugged me tight. He whispered to me, "You crawled before you walked and when you stumbled to your knees there was someone who picked you up. Stumbling is not failure my child. It's only a deterrent to slow you down." He gently held me back away from him and motioned me aside of him. He held out his hands freely to the air and said, "All is given in love and all is taken in love." With those words he stood and began to walk away.

I was crying and couldn't speak. I sat as a frozen statue digesting all Charlie's words. I watched as his frail body and slow moving feet rustled up and down the loose rock.

Once he had reached the top of the Cliffside, he turned and yelled out, "Praise God!" His presence left me just as mysteriously as he had arrived

I left the Cliffside with a new found friend and an eagerness to live triumphantly.

Over the next few days I began to gather up driftwood along with odd and end things that I thought could be of use such as nets, bottles, picnic dishes, towels, clothing articles, flat rocks and more stuff that the tides would bring in. I began to create fishing nets, a bed and a dinner table. I would work on my housing project until early afternoon then I would attend a church service that was held across the highway at a much larger beach park. Homeless people from all over the North Shore would gather under the palm trees in a circle to hold hands in prayer. We would sing and tell of the Bible as we worshipped and praised God. Afterwards, we would socialize in smaller groups and share experiences. Then I would head back to my "beach house."

Once I arrived home, the first thing that I would do was pull up the nets to see what was for dinner. I was always able to find lighters that people lost to keep my fire starting easier. I'd boil water on an open fire and add shrimp, crab, lobster or whatever I would catch the most of. Seaweed was plentiful and mixed in well with every meal. I would sit at the neatly stacked stones that I labeled as a table to eat as the sun went down. When I finished eating, I carried my dishes down to the water to wash. With the use of heavy saturated sand the oils would come right off the plastic dishes and be ready for the next day.

I sat by the open fire at night and admired the sunsets. Sometimes it would appear as if scattered blazes of fire swooped through the skies. Other times it was almost like a dreary desert scene that contained a cactus look. I would lay back and cover with a towel, which served as a blanket at night. The ocean waves breaking against the Cliffside was like an orchestra playing Mozart. The waters were soothing but yet held a significant terror of strength. I kept a beer bottle on the table with collected bird feathers. The feathers symbolized fresh wild flowers and their blossoming growth.

The morning sunrise would faithfully wake me and sleepy-eyed I'd stumble to the public showers to rinse off before the beach area became busy with people. Taking a bath fully clothed was always a challenge.

The day's events were routine but always held something new. I'd comb the beach like a scavenger in search of what may be of use that washed up during the night.

Winter had left with spring coming to an end. I had somehow obtained a small sense of tranquility, love and surrender. Definitely I had an appreciation of simplicity and the elegance that lied within the natural beauty of life. Although I was lonely and heartbroken, it was manageable.

My court date was approaching quickly. I still hadn't found anything to wear that was suitable for the occasion. Suddenly, I noticed a bundle of color that lied just ahead of me. With excitement I ran towards the pile and discovered a newly found moo-moo dress. With thankful tears I held it up and let the wind blow the sand from it. Just off to the side was a mix-match pair of slippers. Different colors but the right feet. I was pleased. I looked up to heaven and expressed my gratitude.

Every day was a challenge to meet basic daily living needs. Sometimes I'd get so frustrated and overwhelmed that I would just kick the garbage container and scream at it insensibly. Yet, other times, was as if I were a glutton for creativity. I couldn't allow my heartache to swallow up my energy.

I would take time to play in the ocean and the sand. I built lighthouses in the sand and pretend that my prince charming would arrive by ship and rescue me. While other times were filled with images of children's laughter echoing throughout the house and I was the mommy. I was lonely and impaired with emptiness. My heart longed for my children and stored vengeance for their father.

Several days passed and I had decided to leave for Honolulu the day before the hearing so as not to be late. I had to meet with an attorney appointed to me by the court prior to the hearing as well. I felt very uneasy thinking about court. I put the thoughts on hold and proceeded with an early dinner. I changed my clothes and put on the moo-moo dress. I dug up the loose change I had collected and hidden over the past months. When I had finished putting away all my things out of view, I started walking away.

I walked down a dusty road that connected to the main road to town. It took most of the afternoon to get into town and the whole time I kept having a reoccurring uneasy feeling of not returning. There was nothing really specific just a peculiar feeling. I finally arrived in Wahiawa. Tired and worn out, I went to the nearest bus-stop bench and flopped down. I sat and waited patiently for the bus to arrive. I people watched and distinctively I recalled wanting to be anyone of them. I wanted to be anyone but me. With great sadness I pushed back the tears. The urge to run back to my "beach house" had grown strong. The "beach house" held a certain security for me that I had developed a peculiar fondness for. Faithfully the bus arrived on time and with slight hesitation I climbed aboard.

I chose a seat next to the window and sat quietly. I stared out the window at stores, malls and restaurants that I used to enjoy but the opportunities had become no longer an option for me. The reminiscing had given me an uneasy sadness. I turned my thoughts to images of my children. I missed them tremendously and I had to find a way to be with them.

The bus finally came to a complete stop. We arrived in Honolulu. I was in no hurry, so I just sat and gathered my thoughts while others departed the bus. Eventually I got off the bus and standing as if I was embedded into the sidewalk I wondered what to do next. I had twelve hours to wait for my lawyer and the court hearing.

I spent the day walking around the city. The closer it got into the evening hours the more I stayed around the beach area. From time-to-time I would stop to listen to the music that entertained the tourists. I was like a lost child wandering the streets in search of a parent. I was sad, lonely and scared.

I found some fallen coconuts and cracked one of them open to drink the milk. I savored the taste of the milk as I sat down and stretched my legs out and leaned back against the tree to take a restful moment. The grass was soft and the aroma of the fresh scent of lavender eased my anxiety. I stuck the extra coconut in my pocket and put a few apple-bananas in another one.

The beaches were becoming deserted of tourists. Finally darkness settled in. The ocean was extraordinary calm that night. The skies deep blue shared its space with the shiniest stars dancing about. The sounds of the ocean waves playing in the background finished creating the serene moment that I needed to lose my sorrow to. I peeled back a banana and thought about wildflower fields as I walked along the waterline.

I would sit for awhile and walk awhile. I noticed a nearby lookout so I headed up the bank of steps that led the way. It was extremely dark at the top of the cliff and the moonlight was dim. I lay down on a bench as if it were my bed and slept peacefully.

I woke up during the night and the shadows that hid the moonlight earlier had faded and allowed the brightness to shine through. The tall peek provided an awesome view of the beach areas of Honolulu. I sat alone and cried with fear of what the morning light might bring. I anticipated a dreary day coming. I had to detour my thoughts so I got up and walked to the edge to look over the area. The only people in sight were obvious lovers in the shadows of the moon. I cried for the longing of a love I never shared with my husband. I sighed and wiped away the tears and wondered why I was so unlovable. I walked back over to the bench and eased myself down in slow motion. I had to do away with the haunting thought of never being in love. I laid down on the bench and stared at the stars and found a real bright star that appeared to be nestled in the realms of clouds as if it was just waiting. I was that star I said to myself. I will be waiting and shining bright one day and some tall handsome heartthrob will notice me. I smiled and breathed in the midnight air. I closed my eyes and went back to sleep. I dreamed of the night I would fall in love and share a single star.

I was awakened by unfamiliar noises. The sun was starting to come up. I yawned and stretched then hurriedly headed down the steps. I had to get through the main stretch of Honolulu before the streets got too crowded and slowed me down. I didn't want to be late for my appointment with the attorney. "I'm going to see my girls today," I shouted aloud with a joyful heart.

The streets were being invaded by well-dressed men and women going to work. They would purposely snarl at me as I walked steadily by. "Look at her," I heard some ladies say to each other as they'd giggle and stared at me. The words that I had overheard made me feel ashamed and my eyes filled with tears. I felt self-conscious, so I picked up the pace and soon after could see the courthouse in full view. I darted in between two buildings to catch my breath and give myself a look over.

I was about two blocks away from the courthouse and heard a familiar voice. I glanced around and saw my husband in the arms of the same brunette that been at my house the day I was removed from the premises. They giggled like school kids as they exchanged kisses on the cheek. I asked myself when would he ever stop publicly humiliating me? I waited to come out of hiding until I knew they had passed by me completely.

Abruptly I entered the revolving door to the courthouse. Oh no! My long moo-moo had got caught in the door and it was still moving!

"Help," I yelled in a high pitched tone.

A man from the desk turned off the power to the door immediately and quickly came to my rescue. Twisting and turning mixed with a lot of tugging and pulling he was able to get my dress tail loose from the door. I extended my appreciation and headed up the stairs. I entered the corridor of the upstairs courtrooms and there stood my husband with his friend. She clung to his arm and they both waved a grand hello to me. The gesture angered me. I couldn't understand why he had always felt the need to flaunt his women in front of me. I had tolerated it through our entire marriage but why was he still doing it? Whatever, I thought. I was too preoccupied with meeting with my lawyer to concern myself with his affairs.

I waited by the window at the end of the hall for the arrival of my attorney. Upon his arrival we exchanged names and all he had to say was "No need to worry and don't get mad. Remain calm at all times."

We entered the courtroom and proceeded to the table located to the right of my husband and his girlfriend.

Court came to order and the judge didn't seem to be all that friendly. He had asked a bunch of questions to the plaintiff but I didn't pay that close attention. The answers kept coming as if he was reading a book. I couldn't concentrate and was at a high level of frustration and anxiety. I didn't absorb much of what had been said except for the individual words that stuck out in my mind. For instance: crazy, alcoholic, violent and paranoid. I looked at my lawyer and he just continued to sit and flip through papers. I nudged him and he just gave me a hush sign. My face was flushed and I was angry but when I heard that girlfriend of his say that I was unstable, I immediately became unglued.

I jumped from my seat and began to yell as I flipped up the table that sat in front of my attorney and I. Papers scattered through the air freely landing all over the floor. The judge continuously banged his anvil. I was wrestled to the floor by the bailiff and the officers that stood about the room, needless to say handcuffed and placed in a chair beside the bailiff. The judge gave me a warning and remarked that he would deal with my jail time after the divorce hearing was completed. The judge continued with what he considered as division of property. The vehicles, money, household possessions and custody of the children were to be awarded to the plaintiff. I got furious and flew off with another tangent, this time cussing the judge. I was under a lot of pressure and I became outraged at the wrong time. The judge sentenced me to eighteen months and one year probate period.

I had displayed every accusation my husband was claiming. How foolishly I fell into his trap that he set before me. He had ripped my heart out and I helped him to do it. Momentarily I felt as if nothing mattered but in actuality I was hurt, scared, defenseless and above all longed for my children. I was dying inside and wanted my husband to hurt just as much as he had hurt me. After all, in my own way I did love this man as much as I possibly could in my own way even though it wasn't the way he thought I should have. It was the best I could do and he betrays me as if I were nothing.

I was still handcuffed so they just shackled my ankles and lead me away to a holding cell in the basement of the courthouse, which is where I remained until the next morning. The cell was overcrowded with women. There were only two long benches attached to the back wall so most of us sat on the cold hard cement floor. It was to be a long night ahead.

When morning came, I was transferred to the jail for processing. I measured five foot four inches and weighed in at ninety-six pounds. There was an adjacent room where I was instructed to remove my clothing. I then was taken to another room where an officer and nurse did a complete body cavity search. It was absolutely humiliating and painful. The workers made crude comments in regards to my body and the females that stood in line behind me added their derogatory remarks. I would yell back at them, but all it got me was a direct blow from the guard's knight-stick that stood off to the side. The stick she carried drew blood from back and legs. My knees buckled and I nearly fell to the floor. Then off to the showers we went. I was too weak to stand so the guards sprayed me with a water hose and called it a shower. I was then photographed and given a jumpsuit to wear and told that there was only one more in my size to not get this one dirty.

I was taken to a private cell after the in processing was completed. I climbed to the top bunk and hid myself against the wall. Scared and crying I lied motionless until late that night. I was awakened by cries of other women and their rigid screams. Women banged ferociously on the bars all night. I just wanted to go back to "my beach house."

The next morning the guards came to escort everyone to a chow line. The food looked unappealing so I gave it back. Immediately after each meal we were taken to a courtyard for what was entitled as recreation. It was a plain enclosed bricked square area with no grass. There was one basketball hoop and several chained down cement benches. The overhead was open and you could see the blue sky and hear the sound of the ocean nearby. The smell of the fresh air scented with salt water was the most serene combination even if it were just for a moment.

The first day in the courtyard I was pushed around and bullied to the degree that I received a broken nose. Within a two-month period, I had withstood several black eyes, cuts and severe bruising. I was beaten on a regular basis--twice a day and even once got a broken arm. I spent a lot of time in the infirmary.

The worst beaten was to near unconscious level. I had multiple contusions and wounds to the head with a severe concussion. I was in the infirmary for a week. During that stay one of the guards befriended me and told me I would have to start defending myself or the women were going to kill me. She also included that I needed to start eating on a regular basis and exercise daily. I was also instructed to let go of anything or anyone that wasn't behind the prison walls that I now resided in.

For a smoother transition I was taken back to my cell during mealtime. I had been given a cellmate and in my absence she overtook my bunk. I knew when she returned from chow that there was going to be a confrontation. I had to prepare myself. I wasn't completely healed and still very sore and wobbly. Most of the women were two to three times bigger than me and stronger as well. I sat and wondered where my advantages lied and it came to me. The inmates didn't know my vulnerable points and if I was ever going to be left alone I was going to have to succeed with the upcoming confrontation.

Chow time was over and you could hear the women chaotically arriving back to the cell block. I was scared but I knew that the confrontation was going to have to start before my cellmate came through the doorway. I sat up on my bunk and waited. She turned her back towards me to talk to someone that stayed further down from our cell and I leaped on her. She fell off balance and I quickly forced her arm between the steel bars on the door. She was at my mercy and I had her full attention. After all, I just wanted to talk to her not fight with her. She screamed and begged for me to let her go. I looked around at the other inmates and let it be known that my bunk would occupy only me and the next time someone decides to throw hands with me that it wasn't going to be settled as nicely as this one was. I kept applying pressure to the girl's arm and amazed how quickly someone is ready to submit to reasonable request.

I got my bunk space and applauded by the other inmates but above all respect was earned. The girl gave her word that there would be no more trouble and somehow I believed her. I was referred to as "the little one" every day after that.

Prison life was a world of its own and had its own rules to survive and live by. It was a definite world of loneliness and disparity.

I laid in bed at night sobbing without tears being shed. I couldn't let anyone know that I was scared or lonely for the scared was beaten and the lonely was raped. It was almost like turning off the light switch however it was emotions you had to click off and on.

Every night was sleepless and a mixture of reoccurring nightmares. I laid awake thru the midnight hours reminiscing over my marriage. I was so angry and hurt that he felt like he could just toss me aside as if I was nothing. I might not have surrendered my soul to him but I did have a fondness for him and was sure to always display respect and gratitude towards him with loyalty. For years I had tolerated his sarcasm of my appearance and his nagging over the obsession I had with being a clean freak. His indecent behavior with women was flaunted at me continuously. As a result of his affairs he had a child with another woman and I even took on the responsibility of the child as if he were one of my girls. Above all the things he would do to deliberately to hurt my feelings was the constant act of comparing me to other women and his mother .The worst thing he could ever say to me was "I would have treated you differently if I would have known all he facts but why couldn't he anyway treated me better if he himself loved me?" The echo of his words rang through my head some nights as if they were repetition chimes sounding and I would cry then get bitter inside my heart.

The humiliating remarks were so clever that most of the time I stayed in turmoil of the person I should be and who I was and would find myself apologizing to him for his actions. It was a marriage of convenience that turned into daily forgiving and not of love, romance, support and kindness. The realization that I had never known what it was like to be loved was hard to swallow but then again did I know how to love anyone other than my children. I never questioned my ability to love as a mother but I had real anger on loving as a woman. I honestly believed as long as I did the things wives were expected to do such as take care of kids, cook, clean and be polite and obedient that a marriage was good. I filled the duties but only as a routine act and he did his role by providing. In all actual reality we lived in a home where there was no love or appreciation about.

The haunting of never knowing love kept my dreams in a nightmare of the past and I never wanted to close my eyes. I would fight off the eerie thoughts so often that it was a constant battlefield in my head. My images of my girls is where I obtained the energy I relied on to get me through days, nights and even moments.

Months passed and life in a cell block had become somewhat manageable. I spent most of the time in anger and social management classes. I had one-on-one therapy sessions three times a week. Saturday evenings were spent at chapel services. I was promoted with good behavior to earn the right to clean the hallways and shower stalls. I always looked forward to Fridays and Sundays so I could have alone time. I went to the facility library while most inmates went to visit with family and friends. I didn't have either so visitation hours were never any of my concern.

One early morning I was wakened by a guard yelling at me, "get packed it's January 28, 1989, and your time has been served."

I didn't have anything to pack so I just sat motionless on my two inch foam mattress that had become my king-sized bed. I was over abundantly scared. The first two processed thoughts were: what do I do next and where do I go? Wow! My stay was over and I didn't realize it.

I was startled by the sound of two guards unlocking the steel barred door that had kept me enclosed and at times even safe. I had grown accustomed to the sound shutting behind me and I would have reassurance but tonight I wouldn't be hearing it. Startled once more from my thoughts one of the guards motioned for me to come towards her and to stand in the doorway. The other guard that occupied the space with me inside the cell handcuffed me and shackled me before she led me through the doorway. They led me down the hallway and the coldness that I once had felt among the same very walls now brought wholesome warmth that I would be leaving behind. Some of the same very girls that were responsible for my beatings months prior were now hollering 'good luck' at me and wishing me well. I nodded as my eyes filled with tears. The most sincere love I had found in life I had discovered behind the prison walls that had housed us all as family. I was being let out of jail and scared to death of leaving.

We entered the halls that were just outside the cellblocks where I had just cleaned the day before. The smells of pine-sol still lingered in the air and the shine reflected our shadows as if we were walking next to a mirror. I might not have been able to do a lot of things but I sure could clean!

We stopped at a clerk's window so the officers could talk and I stood to the side of them lost in my own thoughts. One of the guards turned towards me and put a small package in my hands and announced she would take me to the shower stall soon.

Once the ladies had finished official business at the desk they walked me down to a private shower room. They unlocked my restraints and offered me a seat on a bench next to them. My tears fell, poured out of me like a running water faucet with fear, regret, loneliness and gratitude. I opened the package and it was the moo-moo that I had worn to that dreadful divorce court hearing of what now seemed so long ago. I asked if I could shower before dressing because I didn't know when the next shower was going to be feasible.

She nodded and replied, "Yes, Little One, you deserve it and we will extend you some privacy."

The guards then stepped out to the hallway and I indulged myself in bathing. I finally got out and dried off with my jumpsuit and changed into the moo-moo and mix-matched slippers. I combed my long chocolate brown hair with my fingertips as I had become accustomed to do. The tears kept falling from my eyes non-stop. Once again I was terrified of the unknown. Jail had become the oasis from the storm and now I had to leave it.

I took a deep sigh and washed up my face and decided that it was time to take that leap of faith and the steps towards the door was the beginning.

I touched the guard on the arm and said quietly, "Thank you. I am ready." We headed towards a solid steel door that opened with a buzzard from the desk clerk's office and as it opened I stood realizing I would be on the other side of the door soon. I became overwhelmed with the ideas of what comes next.

A guard interrupted my distant thoughts. "Here is the $240.00 in state funds you have accumulated. It's not much but it will help." She paused momentarily to take a look through some papers that lay in front of her. "You are to report to the probation department on South C Street tomorrow anytime before one o'clock."

"Yes, m'am I understand and will be there first thing in the morning."

We all four exchanged good-bye's as the exit steel door was buzzed open.

I froze still as if time had ceased to exist. I was overwhelmed with what to do next. I looked through the glass window and saw the heavy winter rainfall and unpleasant thought of no place to go on a gloomy rainy day just didn't make for a pleasant release to freedom. My eyes filled with tears and my heart ached with mixed emotions as I stepped towards the door and stopped. I turned towards the guards that had befriended me during my stay and waved.

I turned back towards the door still hesitating because I just wasn't in a hurry to face nothing and that's what awaited my immediate departure. Nothing! I had neither courage nor the gumption in me to proceed.

Suddenly I felt a nudge on my shoulders and encouraging words, "Little girl, this all has been for something and you have a life waiting for you to begin it."

I hugged the woman's neck and cried a moment then I finished stepping through the freedom exit.

The winter air was brisk and the rain was heavy and hard. I stood underneath the overhang and tried to figure out which direction to go in order to stay close for my morning appointment.

I had about nine hours until nightfall. Where is the least congested area that's nearby where I could seek shelter from the stormy rain?

The zoo! It was cheap too for local residents but I couldn't get caught was the only drawback. I dodged rain for nearly eight blocks before arriving at the gate entrance.

It was nearly closing time so it wasn't crowded. I stayed very secluded and kept a low profile until the park gates were closed. The zoo had many pleasant memories for me. It was one of my favorite places to go no matter what city I went to throughout the States.

I located the main concession area and chose the nearby bathroom to stay in for the night. It would be the perfect place due to amount of employees coming in the morning the noise would be sure to awaken me.

I stayed very secluded and kept a low profile until the entrance gates were closed. Then I hid behind a tree until I seen the last employee leave the concession area. I quickly ducked into the bathroom to settle in for a nap and to stay dry from the rain.

I began to play my memory tape of thoughts that had been pause for the past year and a half of my children and family. I cried like a hungry infant wanting to be nursed. I missed my children and wanted nothing more than to have them cuddled up on the couch with me and telling stories to them that I would make up as the story unfolded. I only wanted to be near them. I missed my parents and only hoped that they would understand my absence from them. There was nothing they could do to help me and revealing one more life failure was more than I could bear. I said prayers aloud for all of those I loved and asked for the guidance and protection of the Lord.

I stood at the sink and used most of the paper towels and the automatic hand dryer to dry my clothes from the rain. I stared into the mirror and could see the reflection of scattered sadness taking a toll on me. Where did that little golden blonde girl go that used to meet me in the mirror so long ago?

I called it a night and huddled in the corner by the doorway. The floor had been freshly cleaned and smelled of pine. It reminded me of the first night I had spent in my prison cell: eerie, lonely and cold. Then I recalled the peace I had obtained through its endurance and I knew somehow that better days were coming. I cried myself into a restless sleep and dreamt of the wildflower fields and the deep valley that held it together.

I woke just before sunrise and washed up in the sink. Then I walked the zoo grounds freely until I found a gate that I could slip out of. Being small and anorexic had a great advantage for once. Needless to say, I was successful.

I walked around the streets of Waikiki thinking of a plan to tell my P.O. and kept coming up with nothing. The truth of the matter was I didn't know what I was going to do so I just figured the plan would derive on its own as we talked. Meanwhile I wanted some apple-bananas that I loved so much and knew where a tree was that had a bountiful supply and a tall glass of kiwi juice. I looked in my pocket and was pleased to know that I had a dollar for juice and the fruit was free so I was in good shape for breakfast.

I walked through the beach areas and stopped at one of the sunrise cabana bars and got my juice. The early morning fresh sea air was a soothing spirit that always calmed my worries and cares. The waves were my anchor for daily provisions. The beauty in the depths of the water was the serenity of the deepest need and would echo its love through its currents. I finally located a tree and picked a handful of bananas and sat down on a bench in ocean sight.

Enjoying my hearty light breakfast I recalled my "beach house" and I wanted to go back to the North Shore. It was simple. I would tell the P.O. I was staying with friends and secretively go back to my previous dwelling.

I walked twelve blocks to the address that had been provided to me and waited until they were open. I was anxious to meet with my probation officer.

The doors eventually opened and I entered gracefully. I asked for the person assigned to my case and had a seat in the waiting area.

It was a short meeting that took place in the lobby.

"Call in twice a week to let me know your where-a-bouts. I wish you luck and don't get into trouble. If you do so happen to find yourself arrested, have the jailer to notify me and here is my card." He stood and extended a farewell.

"Yes sir, I understand completely and will comply." I was so relieved to find that the meeting was so informal and I left with a plan in motion.

I got to the bus stop just as it had arrived and boarded the same bus that had dropped me off many months prior. I looked out that window and giving the city a glad riddance, I left the city behind and closed the door to its memory.

I had decided to take my money and buy some camping supplies and a bicycle. I was returning home and had fear but with added contentment because I knew that 'this too shall pass'. I was only paving the destiny to get to my children. I was going to be okay.

I slept all the way to Wahiawa and the driver sent someone back to wake me up. I extended my gratitude as I exited the bus. The adventure was about to enter the next stage.

I excitedly went to the second hand store and bought a raft, tent, metal dishes and a blanket. Then I went to the surplus store and got a backpack and filled it up with all my supplies. Then I headed down the sidewalk to look for a cheap bike however I found a much better deal. Someone had discarded one in the trash down an offside alleyway. I claimed it and went to get a patch kit for the tires and an extra inter tube. It was like new and would do fine for transportation. I still had money left and room in my backpack so I went to the grocery store to get rice, oil and flour. My ambition grew with each stop I had made.

I recalled some words that old man Charlie said to me many months ago on the Cliffside and I repeated them aloud as to hear them, "The fear was alive and the dangers that lay ahead of me were real."

"I am coming home Charlie. Come and visit." I said aloud.

I climbed on my bike and rode out of town when I saw a sign hammered into the ground not far from town that read: FREE CLOTHES. I needed some clothing definitely and I also needed the rest so I stopped and asked if they might have something that I could use and with a smile the kind old woman invited me into her home.

She fixed us a glass of iced tea and brought out a platter of fresh fruit and crackers. We small talked about how she accumulates so much stuff and gives it away. She helped me sort through boxes and bags for clothing articles and then we went to the porch to sit and talk some more. She mentioned she once had a friend named Charlie. I was shocked and listened to her share stories of their friendship.

I asked her to describe him and excitedly interrupted her to tell her that I knew him too. The kind woman rose from the table and went to the other room but only to return with a small box and a sad expression showed on her face.

She said, "Charlie gave me this box and told me you would be passing by this way one day and to give it to you when you came. Charlie spoke highly of you and wanted you to have what little he had. Charlie died two months ago." She was real quiet after that and eventually continued in a soft tone, "if you need me I will be in the next room." She stood and glared at me for a moment then left the room.

I only nodded.

I cried and this time it was for love of a friend. The tears were gentle and smooth and released with sadness. Charlie had given me a profound spiritual awakening. I missed him already. After a few moments spent in silence, I opened the box he had left for me. I held the red plaid coat with an abundance of pockets that he wore the day we had met in my hands. I held it up close to me for it offered his warmth of kindness. I recalled his firm compassion and his excitement for heavenly views. I felt his knife in one of the pockets and took it out to see that it was wrapped in a note. My eyes filled up with tears as I read the words he wrote to me: Little girl, participate in your life by living it and always stop to listen to the music floating in the air and I will see you again one day.

I gave the kind woman a thank you and packed up my belongings to head out to the North Shores of Hawaii to my 'beach house'.

I mumbled under my breath, "I'm going home," someday and started singing old hymns as I peddled down the dirt road.

Upon my arrival to my 'beach house' on the North Shore a large family gathering was taking place. The children were playing and jumping about. Musical instruments were being played by the men as the older women performed traditional hula dances. Then my eyes widened to a feast that was laid out across several tables and the aroma of a roasting boar was mouthwatering. They all seemed happy and extended an invitation to me to join them.

I accepted and played ball with the kids. We would chase each other up and down the shore and whoever caught the ball got buried in the sand. It was so nice and refreshing to laugh and be a part of wholesome fun and relaxation.

The day was coming to an end and they hadn't started to pack up their belongings. The men only threw more wood on the fire. The husband and wife asked me to join them for a walk on the beach. They began to explain to me that they too were homeless. They worked during the day and at night they all slept in the family bus. I was welcomed to stay near and they would help me. They explained that they knew I was a friend of Charlie's and that he would want them to help me. That night I lay under the open skies and was kept warm by the campfire. I was devoured by thoughts of a peaceful confusion and slept very well.

Early morning came and the mother of the children and I took the kids to the public showers to prepare them for school. Meanwhile the men were back at the bus getting ready for work.

I returned to the campsite and dressed in a nice pair of dress pants and flowered blouse to go search for work. Persistence finally paid off. After several hours of searching endlessly I finally found a job that afternoon and would be reporting to work in three days. I was ecstatic!

I went back to the beach and began to settle in. I dug out holes in the sand behind the boulders to place my personal belongings in. Then I dug out a large whole for a bed and lined it with my sleeping bag and placed small rocks around it to keep out loose sand. I built my table and unpacked cooking supplies. I would work and contribute to the cost of groceries and save the rest for plane fare back to the Mainland.

Six months passed and I was released early from probation. I immediately began to count my money and I had just enough to purchase my flight ticket. I was excited! I was going to see my children and family after nearly three years.

The next day I had my local friend to take me to Honolulu to make the purchase of a one-way ticket and that night we ate a feast of victory and danced a farewell hula. The great-grandmother made me a fresh lei and presented it to me with love from the family. Sitting by the open camp fire we reminisced over the past months and said our good-byes. Tears were shared and hugs were exchanged with plenty of laughter shared.

That night after everyone had gone to bed I lit candles and set them assail in the memory of my old friend, Charlie and for my local family. I said a prayer for each one to be blessed and filled with love and to prosper in their earthly lives and in their heavenly lives. I pondered over random thoughts of my life and came to a realization that I had spent most of my life sad, scared and running away. I lit a candle for my loss and then another candle for the newly found peace that I had gained within. I watched as the waves carried the silent request for my life to be as bold as the sea and surrounded with content and admiration of truth.

The next morning the family took me to the airport to catch my flight. We cried some and exchanged aloha's. I boarded the plane with just my coat as my only baggage and the rest of my belongings I had given to my newly found local family. Once I had boarded the plane I waved from the window one more time and took a deep sigh. I tried to think clearly but my mind was too crowded with too many thoughts.

I shifted comfortably in my seat and began to sort my mixed emotions one-by-one. The Islands had brought me much sadness but in return restored my faith and soul. I recalled the memory of the old man Charlie and his words of comfort and how I was able to conquer my fears with just spoken words aloud. I felt protected with a warm spirit as I departed the Islands.

It was fall of 1989 and time to lay to rest the previous years. Although I had many devastating challenges, I survived with love and kindness. My dignity restored and a new development of love, uplifting humility and gratitude made me a success. Those were the years that I would always remember as refining my character to make me a better person. I now had peace amongst the pieces.

The time I spent surviving had come to a closure and I was ready to move on with whatever life had waiting for me. I closed my eyes and nestled in my seat to enjoy a long plane ride.

# Chapter Seven

TWELVE-HOUR FLIGHTS ARE JUST too long.

I was extremely anxious to see my baby girls and just cradle them up in my arms. I made a phone call to their father that night upon arrival to my parent's home. Without engaging in a lot of small talk I was direct and to the point.

"I will be picking up my girls this coming Friday afternoon after school."

"We will see what we can do to have them ready." He replied with hesitation.

Excited and eager I hung up quickly and began thinking of all the things we could do. I tossed ideas throughout my mind until I was in a deep sleep.

Friday finally came and I made the drive across town to get my children.

I knocked on the door with the same vision of my babies tugging on my legs so long ago and I just wanted to scoop them up and love them all. I could hardly wait for their sloppy kisses. However, I was greeted by a strange woman with my babies hiding behind her calling her 'mommy'.

So much had changed.

My youngest could walk and was potty-trained. She had an outstanding vocabulary.

The next to the youngest had started kindergarten and could read simple child story books.

The middle child was learning to cook and had turned into a young teen with dreams and ambitions.

My oldest had boyfriends and had turned into a young lady.

Time had moved on and I missed it all. While I held on to an embedded image of my babies they were growing up and I had become the stranger to them.

My heart broke into a million pieces that day for all the growing years that I had missed with my babies. I cried an ocean of tears that gloomy dreary day.

I made countless attempts over the next following months to reach them as their mother. I wanted them to know desperately how much I loved them. I failed miserably with being able to have them connect with me.

The feedback I received from their father and stepmother was devastating to me. They would tell me how my children would scream for hours before my arrival and have nightmares after they had spent time with me. Repeatedly I would listen to the accusations of how my presence created a negative impact on my children and that I was a major disturbance in their security.

I was overwhelmed by it all. I only wanted my girls to be happy, safe and secure. Above all I wanted them to be loved.

I knew I had to do something but I was torn apart with the only two choices that I had: (1) step back and let them continue in the family they had grown to love and admire or (2) be selfish with the love I held as their mother and tare them from what they knew.

All the signs they displaced when they were with me backed the stories I received from their parents.

After a year and a half and careful consideration, I decided it was in their best interest that I removed myself and allow their father and new wife to raise them until they were older.

I held tight to an image of hope that my young ladies would grow up wanting and needing their mother. With each passing year I was crucified more and more and finally the award winner of the worst person who ever lived.

I carried with me for many years a heavy hearted guilt for the day I moved away and began a new life and with me I took a heavy lonely heart.

The winter of 1990 had been had brought me to an extremely hard decision to face and I believed I did the right thing by them since I couldn't give them the home they needed. Today, years later, given the same surrounding circumstances I would make the same choice again.

I had spent several years off and on in therapy sessions but I always felt unconnected with myself somehow. Realizing that I needed something more, I searched for a specialized therapist in sexual abuse simply because I was unable to identify with being a woman. Something was missing inside of me and I just didn't feel as though as I were a complete individual. I had a yearning to discover the missing link. Furthermore, the fact that I still was unable to recall my childhood like other folks could still lay restless within me. I had established a peace within but I wanted serenity.

Many months I attended group therapy sessions and one-on-one sessions then the day came that I requested hypnotic therapy. The most devastating shock was revealed from deep within my hidden inner closet. I had been molested at the age of four by my grandfather and it had continued until I was nine. That was the missing link that had stood in my way of being complete. The freedom that I received from that dark deep hurt soared from me as if I was a baby eagle leaving the nest. I continued to participate intensively with my therapist and grew emotionally stronger each day thereafter. I began to lose resentment, hate and bitterness that resided beneath the heart. I became a compassionate, grateful, kind and above all the desire to love. My ambitions became my reality and I strived everyday to live with a joyful heart.

A few years passed by and I had become more enriched with self-discipline and someone that I was proud to be. But there was a small part of me that clung to the past as if was safety comfort that it hindered me to experience intimacy. With a love desire and intimate desire so strong I was willing to forgive my perpetrators to gain serenity.

Finally I began to work intensely further with my therapist and began forgiving my abusers. I contacted my violators one by one. Those that I couldn't see face-to-face I wrote to and included in my letters all the emotional impact that their actions had caused me but I also included my hopes and dreams to show them that there wasn't an existence of a scared little girl any longer. I closed each letter with hope for their prosperity and redemption. Then I stuffed the letters in balloons and watched the last of my fears, anxieties and pain blow away with the wind. I walked away in dignity.

I have established an extreme gratitude for my life experiences of the dreadful days for without them I would most likely not have found the need for a spiritual guided life nor would I have become a selfless person.

I still had the dream of that special someone. I longed for the day I would share with a soul mate. However, I also accepted that it may be factual that destiny's path didn't have that in store for me. So I went on with my life and settled into a nice predictable secure life in total acceptance that it was a great possibility that I would grow old alone. Then one day unexpectedly it all changed,

I pulled into a gas station and while I pumped my gas the most gorgeous set of eyes I had ever seen met with mine.

"Hi," and the handsome man extended his hand to me, "I am Marlon. Let me pump your gas for you."

"My name is Niveah," I replied in a stutter.

His smile was captivating! I could only focus on his deep set brown eyes and could only faintly hear his soft deepen voice. I stood still in a motionless moment as time seemed to stop. My insides were warm and fuzzy by this handsome man's presence. My feet and hands began to sweat and I lost all sense of the world around me. I wanted to know this gentleman.

He finished pumping my gas for me and I said thank you. He extended his hand to me once more and this time he slipped me a note that read: call me! I want to get to know you. 332-8964.

I called him the next morning and we talked endlessly on random topics. It was conversation that came so naturally and easy. The sound of his voice was intriguing but above all he participated during the conversations. I was outwardly impressed by the fact that he paid attention.

We talked every day thereafter, sharing our personal hopes and dreams for our futures. We talked about everything from death to home values. We were confidants and the best of friends. He gave me an unique contentment about myself and my life.

It was all of my friend's and families opinion that I was certainly falling in love due to the silly awkward things I would do by being dreamy of his presence or even plain ignoring him at times and  they were right I couldn't turn my feeling's away from him. The most memorable thing that I encountered was walking into a wall not long after we had met and I bruised my nose all the way across. I simply adored him!

God had truly blessed me with such a wonderful friend as Marlon.

Our friendship continued to flourish and develop a mutual trust, understanding and devoted companionship. He occupied my every thought throughout the day and was my focus of my dreams. Although our physical attraction to one another remained in our own secret thoughts until one special evening when we sat together admiring a bright moonlit night and he took my hand in his hand and pointed out a lonely drifting star.

"That's me," Marlon said as he pointed to the sky, "and that star over there is you."

He continued saying, "Stars eventually unite together and I hope one day we will too."

I was speechless. My only thought was I must mean as much to him as he does to me.

He turned to me holding my hand gently in his and touched my cheek with the other hand and kissed me. It was soft, gentle and filled with passionate energy. I was left breathless and weak. His eyes glistened while my heart raced faster than a cheetah. I sat speechless as my body's inside filled with a tremble of warmth.

He had always been attentive and intuitive of my needs and compassionately and understandingly fulfilled them. I only needed a validation that he was true and it was his kiss that supported his words and actions.

Months passed with enjoyment pleasure of just knowing that I had a true companion.

One early afternoon I sat in the park admiring the early fall foliage. I pondered over my life and with ease and I thought about Marlon. He occupied my every passing thought and was the focus of my dreams when I laid my head to rest at night. However, somehow, I was at constant battle with myself wanting to share the simplest thoughts and the most complicated thoughts with him for he was a comfort inspiration to me.

I was so blessed and at peace with myself. I had a good life.

Suddenly I was interrupted with a message tone from my phone. It was a text message from Marlon and it read: just thinking of you always and want you in my life, mind, body and soul. I need you to keep loving me the way you do.

I indeed did love him. Tears of joy filled my eyes as I admitted in a text message the same admiration towards him.

Marlon pursued me that day forward as if he were a lion protecting his pride. He held me as if I was rare delicate china. We soared to heights of intimacy that was a complete surrender of our trust and belief in one another.

God not only blessed me with a friend and companion but a soul mate. I trusted Marlon with my every thought and my every breath. I had fallen in love for the first time in my life at the age of 45 and Marlon continues to ravish me everyday. Prayers are always answered and when God sanctions your wants and desires they are above and beyond what you ask for.

# Chapter Eight

A WISE MAN ONCE told me to always remain teachable and the teacher would appear.

Marlon accented my weakness' and encouraged my strength's. I was complete with him as part of my life.

I survived my abusers with clinging to hopes, dreams and fantasies. However, I recovered and participated in my own life with the assistance of outside resources and I pray you do the same. Without help I wouldn't have been able to find the courage to rid my life of pain and would have never known an once-in-a-lifetime love.

We never can know the severity of ones truth but for closed doors to open and truth be revealed there has to be an existence of trust that has no ridicule and judgment. This may be your life or someone you know, prayers be with you.

Help is in a bountiful supply. Seek it and you shall find it. Reach further than the skies and you will obtain it but if you never do anything-nothing is what you will receive.

Though life offers devastation at times we have to accept it to be able to know compassion. Without truth we would never know hope. Our futures are held in today and therefore today will never know an ending. We only have moments. Share them in love.

Niveah stood from her porch swing and wiped a slow trailing tear from her face and bellowed into thin air "God watch over the abused and tormented families and deliver a changed heart to the perpetrators of this world. Guide the abused from behind their closed door's"

Niveah took the last sip from her tea cup and she felt an arm slip about her waistline and the soft kiss on the base of her neck She turned to stare into the loving eyes of her devoted Marlon. The morning began in harmony and content for Niveah and her devoted partner as they watched the dewy mist disappear through the sunlight and the cool mountain breezy air fade away carrying the secret thoughts of Niveah with it.

"Good-morning my Love," he said with another soft kiss planted to my lips.

"Good-morning my Darling," I responded with yet more kisses added.

God only brought me through the broken roads to lead me back home.

Life opened new opportunities once the realization of existing throughout life was not living and it will be for you too. Remember a closed door can't be entered until it's opened!

With love, Niveah.